The Grey Isle Tale

By Ryan P. Freeman

to Josh,

enjoy!

— Ryan P.F.

To contact Ryan by email, send to: thephoenixofredd@aol.com. You can also follow Ryan via social media:

www.facebook.com/
RyanPatrickFreeman
Twitter: @Ryanpfreeman
www.rienspel.blogspot.com
www.rienspel.tumblr.com/

The Grey Isle Tale is dedicated to the refugees of the world – past, current, and future; and also to my friend, Jennie Kelly.

Table of Contents

Preface

The Grey Isle is a place, secluded from the very world upon which it floats. At its center stands Mount Silvertine, rising high above the nearly ever-present fog which rolls in from the sea. The scent of the land is unique, too. One smells the rain mixed with the light, tinging aroma of pine forests. In the air, the salty bite of the sea is inescapable. During the fall the islanders harvest the Trennin apple orchards – which have stood growing in the still air for so long, they are virtually a wood of their own by now. Many peoples have lived there over the vast current of time: the Shining Ones first – next the Elves; then Rumenjians, and finally Rillians. This story is about when the Rumenjians ruled there, already at the crumbling height of their empire.

This is a sort of story which is strange for me to tell. While personally I've had heartaches and true trials I've had to face in my life – I've always been comforted with an abiding trust deep inside about how it will somehow inexplicably work out for good. But it's an easy thing to write niceties like that. It's a far harder thing to live like you actually believe in hope when you wake up in hell one morning. Oftentimes, people eventually wind up in their own self-constructed personal hells... but sometimes hell comes to us. We didn't ask for it or want it – but shadow by building shadow, its empire stretches up, towering over and around us now. We live in it. We are residents. But I think it's important to remember how we don't have to live there. It's not our true home. Even the fact that we can tell that it's horrible means, implicitly, that we know better. It means somewhere deep inside we remember a better place and better ways. We yearn for this... thing... this better thing... way... place. And our aching is transformed into striving. We are a part of a desperate struggle which not even Death himself will one day withhold from us. Better will be one day intimately known to us. (You just wait and see.)

- Ryan

Chapter I

Routine Inspections

The sea-breeze rustled through the pine forest where Janos stood, watching the hazy coastline extend for miles. Here and there, merchant vessels or little fishing boats bobbed along the iron-grey froth of the Ocean Vaste. The metal circlet balanced firmly on his head felt unnatural. Janos constantly had to fight the urge to swipe the damn thing off. He had to also restrain a similar urge with the heavy, overly-encrusted silver sabre hanging from his waist.

"Your highness, are you completed with inspecting the Tower Oros?" asked the local captain.

Janos wracked his mind briefly for her name.... "What was it, again?" his memory had always been terrible. Every so often Janos tried to practice the memory games his etiquette tutor had suggested... but the trouble with forgetfulness is...

"Now what was I thinking about again? ... Hmmm... It's Gisele. Captain Gisele Perrault." Prince Janos remembered with sudden relief. Turning to address the raven-haired captain, he smiled and nodded his approval. "Yes Gis... Captain..." Janos cleared his throat over the etiquette mistake.

Captain Gisele blushed, but still stood like a straight-razor, raptly attentive.

All around them now, the salty sea

winds brushed against their lips and ears. A gust caught in the prince's long cape tangling it in the captain's curly black hair.

Janos fidgeted. He didn't like being embarrassed. Unbidden, the prince could still hear his father's gruff words,

"So long as they're not faction heads from the leading Scypiasians, Ulians or Brutaejians families... it doesn't matter what anyone else thinks." Giving the massive Watch Tower of Oros one last perceptive glance, Janos untangled himself from the captain as best he could and asked, "Forgive me, but you... you're..."

Gisele's reaction confused the prince. She appeared to grimace, flex, and grin all in a flash before quickly masking back behind her usual military poise. "Brutajian, by birth – if you must know – Your Highness." She looked down and away for a moment, "We've been serving as the Watch for this coastline among the Towers since your grandfather, I believe. But I..." Suddenly she leaped at Prince Janos, knocking him flat against the hard timbers of the watchtower's deck. "GET DOWN!"

THUD!

A large ballistae bolt sunk deeply into one of the dark roof beams nearby, still quivering violently.

Captain Gisele's sabre – lean, sharp, and plain was out in a flash. Janos felt a sudden pang of envy as he slowly realized someone had just tried to kill him. "Protect the prince! Soldier, get the Hastati deployed now!" She ordered a nearby guard who was still staring rather shocked at the embedded projectile mere inches from his pale face. Captain Gisele poked her head hesitantly up to peer over the battlements after the stunned soldier finally scurried off obediently...

Thunk Thunk Thunk!

A series of arrow-shots peppered the stonework inches from her face.

"Hastati?!" cried the prince incredulously. "But where are my Imperial Legionaries?"

Down below, the ringing clang of metal on metal drifted up, mingling with the ceaseless rush from the nearby surf below.

"Right now Prince Janos of House Ulian – I don't care if you're used to dragons guarding you! Hastati are what the Ulian family – your family – allows us to garrison here. And we need to move now, because half-trained, conscripted eighteen-year-old Hastati are all we've got at the moment. This way!"

The prince and the captain began crawling towards the entrance to the tower's spiraling staircase. Near the relative safety of the opening, another shower of silvery arrows sailed through the exposed turret's open air deck.

"Ah..." cried Janos... momentarily pinned by his arrow-bitten sleeve.

As Gisele yanked the arrow out and tossed it aside, Janos felt a faint trickle of blood seep down his arm, staining the wood near his boots. "I hope Ulians are made of tougher stuff than that." said the captain with a wry smile, as she half-dragged the prince down into the dark tower.

Onwards they plunged into the dim and the dank of the musty old sea tower. Every now and again, they were forced to flatten against the old stone walls as squads of half-frightened, half-excited recruits jangled past towards the none too distant sounds of fighting. Soon both the prince and the captain could smell the unmistakable odor of burning clashing with the cool coastal air.

Captain Gisele groaned, "Don't tell me the bastards lit the place on fire... my men and I scrubbed this mangy place for a week and a day for your ruddy inspections..."

"My dear captain, I..." began the prince.

"Oh shut up, Your Highness," barked Gisele, brushing a stray lock of dark hair from her face.

Janos looked mildly surprised at the tone this local captain was taking with him. By every right he was her prince, after all. The sentiment was not lost on Gisele, either... "If we live through this you can throw me in the stocks for a week – I really don't care. Right now, I need to find the right brick. Move." Shoving Janos aside she began furiously hitting the stone wall with her free hand. "Well," Gisele said impatiently after Janos continued to stare at her, shocked by this back-water captains' impertinence. "Are you going to help me or not?"

"Sure," said the prince, becoming more and more confused and flustered. Unsummoned, a voice in his head rather like his mother, the Queen, began fussing, "Just imagine it... my son alone and unescorted in the presence of some common Brutajian girl... filthy creatures..." Silencing the internal voice with little difficulty, Janos began hitting the wall at random... though he was still not entirely sure what exactly it was they were looking for in Tower Oros' gloomy, moss-ridden interior.

With an unexpected crunch, the large brick Janos had been pushing slid back into the wall. For a moment, nothing happened. The prince shot the captain a sarcastic look.

"Well... give it a minute," grumbled Gisele impatiently, as she hesitantly sheathed her sword.

Down and around the long, dim corridor the sounds of fighting could be heard clearly now, growing louder with each passing moment.

"I don't think we have a minute, captain."

"Well, it worked just fine last week when I oiled the gears from the other side..."

Finally, with agonizingly slow speed, the wall began creeping sideways, then sliding and swinging inwards, it hitched itself onto some hidden latch. Before the duo lay a billowing, pitch-black tunnel which stank like seaweed. It was all Janos could do from making a face. "I wasn't even aware Oros had a secret passage..." he muttered.

Gisele rolled her dark eyes, "Well... My Prince ... that's sort of the point about secret passages, you know. They're secret," she said exasperatedly, as if explaining sums to a toddler. "Besides... it was the Brutaejians who built these towers a stone at a time... or perhaps their royal majesties, the House of Ulian, have forgotten..."

With a clash and a clatter, two armed men erupted around the far corner of the tower's hallway.

"There HE is!" cried one, brandishing a long silvery spear.

"Friends of yours?" asked the prince apprehensively.

"I was about to ask you the same thing," muttered the captain as they both drew their weapons.

But before either of them could react, a third figure leapt around the corner, tackling the two assassins to the grimy stone floor. With a few swift strokes, the new man whipped out two long steel daggers and slit their throats. After nonchalantly cleaning his bloodied blades on one of the now dead men's cloaks, he gingerly rose from the floor.

"Legate Avors!" cried Prince Janos.

"My Liege! Oh, it is good to see you, sir! I tried to warn you about leaving your bodyguard behind like that..."

The two friends embraced like old comrades.

"How were you not killed, and where are the rest of the men?" asked the prince.

Captain Gisele narrowed her eyes and did not lower her blade, "yes, Legate Avors," she said taking a step closer now, "how exactly did you make it all the way up here unscathed?"

The jarring sounds of fighting were still uncomfortably close. The trio peered down the ominous secret passageway for a moment. The faint torchlight, feeble and groping, did little to illuminate even the entrance's tangle of weedy moss and ancient patchwork stone walls which led on, deeper into the darkness of its own oblivion.

"I'll tell you all once we get moving – your garrison is about to be overrun by Scypiasian soldiers... ninth legion, if I had to guess."

The prince and the captain eyed each other knowingly. It was common knowledge among the realm of the Grey Isle about the legendary fighting abilities of House Scypiasian's ninth legion. "Right," Janos nodded, "Captain, after you."

Gisele rolled her eyes but moved forward despite her obvious mistrust, snatching up a nearby torch off its bracket, and proceeded into the inky tunnel. "One of us has to be the brave one here..." she muttered just loud enough so the other two could still plainly hear.

"What was that, captain?" the legate asked coolly.

"If you two think just because you're of House Ulian you can..."

Prince Janos saw it too, "Avors, you're bleeding – are you sure you're alright?"

The legate looked down at his far side, which had, until this moment been shielded from view. A deep gash seeped with a crimson tide of blood, dripped onto the floor. "I..." Avors tried to speak, but a wave of dizziness swept through him.

The prince caught the soldier just before he toppled over.

"Get him inside before anyone finds us..." barked Gisele, as she sheathed her sword once more.

Together, the pair just managed to drag the imposingly large body of the legate out of the light. The captain tugged at a small inconspicuous lever and the opening re-sealed itself as if it had never existed. The trio was immediately plunged into near pitch dark. The sounds of the last bits of stout resistance appeared to die away... replaced now with new sounds of dripping water and a faraway rush of echoing tide.

"Legate? Avors, can you hear me?" Janos asked worriedly as he forced some wine from his flask down his friend's throat.

Avors choked and spluttered. "It was the ale," he managed finally. "My men were reposing...err... standing guard outside Oro's gates near the courtyard... poisoned. It's..." he coughed again, it's a good thing I was late... eh prince?"

Janos tried to put on a brave smile, "You were double checking the manifests again, weren't you? You worry too much."

The legate grimaced, "not nearly enough, it would seem..."

Through the frail yellow torch light, Gisele could just be seen frowning, "if I patch you up, do you think you can walk?"

Avors nodded. "Get to work, then, captain," he turned again to Janos, "Something's not right... It's been that way for months now. You know it's true... extra supply orders... more armed men on the roads..."

"Yes, legate, I know... It's why we're even out here on the utter edge of the eastern coastlands in the first place... inspecting towers... pah... rubbing shoulders Brutaejians, who would have thought?" Janos joked.

Gisele purposefully cinched the bandage around Avor's waist tight, eliciting a grunt from the legate. "I AM Brutaejian, in case you snotty Ulians forgot. If you would rather I hit that switch and march you both out for all your charming Scypiasian friends to fawn over... What is the third great house of Rumunjia of the Grey Isle doing here at all, anyway?"

Avors took a sharp, painful breath and stood up with a lurch. "I don't know, do I... captain? They're certainly not here for your apple harvest festival in Trennin, that's for sure."

7

Slowly, the group began stumbling down the dim tunnel. After a few minutes, they came to a sudden fork in their path.

"Well Captain Gisele, is it right or left?" the prince asked, suddenly hesitating.

Gisele narrowed her eyes and sheathed her sword. "Look, do you aristocrats even trust me or not? Because last I checked, I did just save your life, legate. AND yours, Your Highness."

Legate Avors narrowed his eyes, "speak in that tone of voice one more time to your prince, brute, and I'll..."

"You'll what, Avors?" asked Janos, "bleed on her?" He took a few steps forward and peered down each identically sable tunnel in turn. "Look, I don't really like it any more than you do. But if it means getting out of here, getting you to a proper doctor or chirgeon... I don't really care. She did save my life. And probably yours, too, my friend."

Avors looked at them doubtfully.

Captain Gisele rolled her eyes, which glistened in the wan torchlight, "my parents did always warn me against strange men..." She picked up two stone from the rocky floor and handed each companion one of them, "Prince, chuck this down the right hallway, if you please – Legate Bleedy, you chuck this down the left one... you nobles do know your rights from your lefts, correct?"

"Why?" they both asked.

"Just do it," she ordered.

"I am *not* Legate Bleedy, you worthless peasan..." retorted Avors, but Prince Janos cut him off.

"Just throw your rock. We all know your real name..." Janos turned to Gisele, still struck by her lovely dark eyes, and winked.

Avors threw his rock down the left chasm, careful to avoid stressing his newly bandaged side. After a few seconds there was a watery crash. The legate sniffed.

"Alright, my turn," said Prince Janos hefting his rock and chucked it down the right corridor. Almost immediately, there followed a noisy skittering sound which died faintly away.

"The right hall way will lead out of the hills to a secret entrance near the edge of Trennin's apple orchards," Captain Gisele explained. "The left has a nasty drop before leading out to our sea-cave. If I had actually wanted to kill you, I would have led you down the left and let you walk right off the edge - if the rocks hadn't of ended you, the breakers would have."

Janos clutched his arm, "oww. Well, I trust you Gisele... but oh... I had forgotten this was the arm the arrow bit me in..."

"My Lord?" asked Avors.

"It's nothing..."

Avors slowly nodded as he began hobbling off, "I'll go investigate the right passageway, then."

"It's nothing, eh?" Gisele said with a smirk Janos could just distinguish through the dark, "take off your shirt."

"Excuse me?"

"You heard me. Take it off. I have to make sure you actually are ok. Seriously... it's a wonder you bumbling Ulians ever made it to power in the first place..."

The prince starred at this upstart Brutaejian captain. In his mind, other voices murmured about the impropriety and breach in correct decorum of the given situation. "It's dark and there's nobody else around..." Janos mentally apologized. Hesitantly, he tugged his laced silk shirt up over his head.

After a moment, he could feel a gentle finger tracing the scars on his chest, "that's not my arm, captain."

"Shut up, my prince. I have to make sure none of the arrows hit you anywhere else... You don't want to end up all loopy like Legate Bleedy..."

There in the dark, the two lingered together. The crash of the breakers still echoed... and still Gisele's surprisingly delicate hands searched out for wounds.

"I saw you once before... you know," she finally managed.

"Is that so, captain?"

Gisele smiled, "once upon a time, your father, the King, had summoned all the captains and advisors to his... or should I say your royal palace of Senokia... all the damsels of the land too... for a royal ball..."

The prince smiled and nodded in the darkness, "my eighteenth birthday party seemed like ages ago... in another life... Why, did we dance or something?"

The captain gave the prince a light shove, "nope. Your royal highness apparently doesn't have time to mingle with peasant brute captains from Oros... oh, but how I watched... and dreamed," her hands slid up to his neck where a curious necklace glittered dimly out of the blackness. "There it is, too."

"What, the Wardstone? Yep, that's it."

"The stone of light which keeps evil at bay – taken from a holy place of the elves of the mainland... given to your family after the liberation of their coastlands beyond the Great Forest," her fingers caressed his neckline until... They were only inches away from each other now. Janos could feel the captain's quivering body next to his... Through the feeble, flickering flames, he caught a glimpse of Gisele's entrancing face once more.

The captain could feel her heart pounding away in her chest. In that moment she knew they were both contemplating the same question, "did they dare?"

Suddenly she gasped and pulled away. In one liquid motion, Captain Gisele whipped out her sword, "GET BACK, CREATURE!"

"Gisele, what's wrong?"

"YOU KNOW WHAT'S WRONG, *MONSTER*."

Prince Janos held up his hands. The buzzing voices in his head grew louder, but with an effort he managed to subdue them. Janos could feel a trickle of moisture where the captain had brushed against the numerous death wounds where his skull connected to his spine, "Gisele, I know how this may seem..."

"So," the captain said as she began circling the prince slowly, "all my men... dead. This was your scheme all along. And I suppose... I suppose the Scypiasians who were attacking my tower were actually good, loyal soldiers, just trying to stop you."

The prince backed against one of the stone walls. The dripping water felt shockingly cold against the smattering of death-wounds which dotted the lower back of his neck and spine. "Gisele, it's not that simple. Please... I..."

Slice.

"Don't you dare call me *Gisele*, you undead... *thing*," with a swift thrust, she drove her sword into the prince's heart.

Janos only smiled softly, as an aching sadness filled his longing eyes. Gently but firmly, he wrenched Gisele's hand away from her sword hilt. With a squelch, he slid the captain's sword out of his chest and calmly cleaned it for her with a spare pocket handkerchief. "Ah captain, if only you could..." and returned Gisele's weapon into her shaking fingers.

The crunch of sand and pebbles announced the return of Legate Avors, "turns out the bloody brute *is* right... there is an exit not far down the right corridor, Your Highness."

Gisele drew back and away from Prince Janos as if splashed by scalding water. Struggling to remain a personally acceptable regal semblance of decorum, Janos struggled awkwardly to pull his shirt back on. The fabric slid down, concealing yet another dribbling death wound just as Avors neared the pair.

"Something the matter, prince?" asked Avors curiously.

"It's nothing," both Janos and Gisele blurted simultaneously.

"Ummm... well, right then. This way," replied the mildly suspicious legate.

...

Together, the trio soon found the exit from the endless crushing night of Tower Oro's secret escape tunnel. Exiting through a particularly dense patch of curtained green ivy, they stumbled out through the ivy-covered cave mouth into the warm light of day. The prince still felt rather sorry for the captain... it was apparent she was still slowly recovering from her shock. The legate, though, trudged onwards, leading the way – politely oblivious as ever.

It wasn't the first time Janos had seen the Five Points during their apple festival. The five nearby towns, or Five Points, which dotted the distant wooded hills, gathered together each autumn in Trennin, the central town nestled in a nearby pleasant, bowl-shaped valley. All around the trio, the orchards, dotted with bountiful red and golden apples, waved serenely in the breeze. Somewhere vaguely behind them, the air still retained its faint sea tang.

The captain scouted the area, moving more on muscle reflex than active will. Prince Janos scared her... terrified her, even. But all the same, she saw the longing sadness in his eyes. Gisele remembered the way she had been smitten by him during the royal dance... how Janos had seemed so far away... inexpressibly distant across the ballroom and layers of social strata. As far as the northern horizon is from the southern... she felt herself sigh.

All was still around her. Gisele forced herself to turn, and reluctantly headed back to where the two men stood, blinking in the buttery afternoon sunshine. "Seems safe enough," she reported neutrally, trying to sneak a glimpse at Janos and failing. Sweeping back her raven black hair, Gisele turned right and started off towards Trennin, soon overtaken by the obstinate legate.

Every now and again, the surrounding silence would be interrupted by the gentle thud where a ripe apple fell to the earth. The group now hurried along the strangely quiet orchard lands, along sun-dappled grounds and past wicker baskets left brimming with the ripe promise of a good harvest. But nowhere was a soul to be seen. The salty wind sighed through the ancient, creaking bows all around them. The band's fears, transformed during their recent underground journey gripped their hearts again with tensile strength once more. A lingering, shadowy omen, invisible, yet all too tangible, dogged their hesitant steps like a specter.

The trio strode through the apple orchard. A crystalline mist was beginning to pool in the little dells all around them now, as the sun at their left began slowly slipping down into the east behind the far distant peak of Mount Silvertine. The captain shivered involuntarily after catching a glimpse of the prince again.

Janos noticed Gisele's shudder and sighed, "you have no idea what it's like, you know."

Gisele pretended not to hear, and picked a ripe yellow apple instead, which glinted in the sun-slanted fog.

Janos's foot hit a loose white paving stone – which sent the hard rock bouncing and skipping along the ruts and roots of the ground in front of them. "I feel... I... I feel this poison coursing through my veins more than my own blood most days. I have to fight the memories of all my worst moments. Always..." The prince stole another glance at the beautiful, rugged captain trudging along a little behind him. For all the two spaces between them – Janos felt in his heart as if the distance of oceans lay between them instead.

After a moment, Gisele squared her firm shoulders and without turning to the prince, replied, "you're wrong."

"Huh?" the prince stopped short.

The captain kept walking past him, on through the dappled sunlight which cut through the wood-shadows of the apple branches dangling high above their heads. "Don't stop. And don't act surprised, either. If you're... infected – then however, whatever it is ... your... melancholy is a part of it, too."

"I... Oh," Janos resumed his shambling pace.

"My father would watch the western seas, you know... I... I don't really know why I'm telling you this, but it doesn't really matter... as a little girl, I would sit on his lap as he watched by the great signal lights... and I would ask him why he watched. And I'll never forget what he would say... my father would say 'We watch in the night not for ourselves, but for others.' I always figured if everyone watched for others, that way we'd all maybe be taken care of one day, you know?"

"Who watches for me, then? Who even would now... considering my condition?"

As quick as lightning, Gisele swiveled and chucked her uneaten apple straight at the prince; Janos, who was still morosely absorbed in his thoughts, failed to duck in time.

Thunk!

The yellow fruit hit him squarely on the nose.

"Ow?" the prince said after a pause. "You know, I don't exactly feel pain anymore." He said as he busied himself with resetting his nose in more or less the right angle.

"Oh, that was for me, Your Highness."

"So I see." Janos replied, patting his face. Satisfied, he shook his head and sighed. The prince couldn't help but smile a little over the captain's quirkiness.

For a time, they trotted onwards, steadily making their way north through the golden mist and endless rows of trees ripe for harvesting. Keeping the sun on their left hand, the prince and the captain eventually caught up to the heavy footfalls of Avors as he went tromping through the flickering leaves and tall auburn grass. "Your Highness, the town is just ahead... they have all gathered for the harvest festival now – which is why the fields are as empty as the gra... are quiet."

"Any sign of the Scypiasians, legate?"

Avors shook his grizzled head, "no, thankfully not. It's odd, though. It's as if nobody here even realizes the extent of what's going on... I don't like it," he turned to Janos, "Sire, we need supplies and news – I need to probably change my wound's dressing and we need to plan our next moves. If you must come into town, I would highly suggest taking great care to disguise yourself."

Janos nodded. He felt the better part of him wishing it really was just a fine autumn festival day here amid the golden apple trees. But the other part of Janos knew better. Almost instinctively, the dark part of his mind whirled with all the negative, sick reasons why they were really here, walking under the misty tree-limbs laden with fruit... Janos caught Captain Gisele's concerned expression. For a moment the two parts of him wavered – both equally balanced as if on the head of a silver pin – and then the brighter part of the prince won over. She was watching for him. Watching and watching like the guiding pinprick of a lighthouse shining out for lost ships upon a midnight sea.

Legate Avors tossed Janos and Gisele a burlap festival shawl each. The Prince caught his own absentmindedly. "When at the Trennin Apple Festival..."

"Do as the Trennians do," finished Gisele, donning her own burlap festival shawl with a grin.

Chapter II

Trennin

The ground continued to rise steadily as the last outliers of the vast orchard faded away, replaced instead by golden fields and rustic farm houses. As the trio crossed over a deep canal, the village proper seemed to spring up all around them. The local excitement of small country towns for their festivals is something special. In a place usually only vaguely remembered for boredom and the steady plodding of daily life, the buzz of Trennin's Apple Festival could have easily been mistaken for a royal visitation. Even Prince Janos could feel the tangible anticipation. The anxious energy was like nothing he could ever have remembered experiencing before during his life at the palace. Official to-do's always utterly bored him because his part always devolved to waving sycophantically, shaking hands with people with hopelessly forgotten names, and dancing with plump strumpets who Janos always noticed bore the distinct impression of either hungry wolves in silk or wide-eyed lambs, silent on their slaughter days.

The bright colors, red, blue, and gold of the fluttering decorations blossomed out of the wooden and tannish-taupe stone buildings cropped up, thick and huddled, on either side of them. After another mile or so of plodding, they began to meet other festival goers – stragglers late for one reason… or excuse… of one sort or another… hurrying along. Soon the trickle of people became a stream and then a river as they neared their destination: Trennin. Most men and women wore their best clothes – or bright engaging costumes drawn from Rumenjian folk heroes like Legate Longinus, famed cavalry commander and founder of their empire; Romestamo the Wizard, long-lived wandering conjurer; or even the ever-imperious Julius Caesar. With a mock gasp, the festival goers sprang aside as a long black snaking form of a wyvern – the ancient name for sea serpent - whisked past, slipping on down the street.

"The Sea Serpent!" squealed little children as they pointed furiously, caught between equal delight and fear.

"Is he real, momma?" another young girl with long dark hair and brown eyes asked, suspiciously.

Janos paused just long enough to catch the perplexed mothers' halting reply, "no... No Hannah, dragons aren't real, dear one. Everyone knows that."

Turning, Janos addressed Avors, "What is it which makes this simple little villa of a town – just an overgrown plantation – so merry... so alive? Is it soil? Weather? Is it family or home?" puzzled the Prince.

Gisele was carefully watching Janos with a guarded, yet curious expression now, as if she were considering him. But her honest face, like a sun passing behind fleeting clouds, soon returned to her steady vigilance, as she scanned the well-trodden road for trouble.

"They know their home is not here, amid the apples – but with the life which grows within them." explained the legate with a bemused smile. Pausing with the prince, they both halted and drank in the warmth of the bright little festival. "My family came from these hills, you know."

The growing crowds thickened as the group neared the town square. One could easily tell this town had been well planned out. Thanks to steady, effective Rumenjian engineering, each of the five roads met, straight as arrows in flight, together at Trennin's exact center. All around, proud marble columns rose up like tall statuesque palm trees, sunny and firm. Looking closer, behind bustling market stalls and merchant stands stuffed with wonderful trinkets, sizzling apples skewered and drizzled with chocolate or honey, life-like art, noisy livestock, local bake sales, shining farming equipment, horses for all occasions, and even purportedly astonishing replicas of the very same jewel now dangling around Janos' neck filled their view. Upon closer inspection, there were even fantastic statues depicting mythical creatures and scenes from all the old Rumenjian tales heralded down from antiquity. Janos, Gisele and Avors had only a few moments to gaze all around, trying their best to see what could have easily taken a dozen more eyes to take in before the local town watch began politely, yet firmly clearing the streets for the upcoming parade.

Shuffling off to the side in order to make way for someone else was an entirely new experience for the prince. At first he just stood there, unmoving. Some overly-trained impulse clearly knew everyone was moving aside for him...

"Janos! Hey, JANOS!" Gisele hissed.

"Oohf," one of the gruffer town guards jabbed the prince with the butt end of his spear.

The prince found himself being guided away from the frowning local watchman, whose eyes followed him as Janos moved away, back into the obscurity of the crowd. It was a wonder Janos had not been recognized... especially after his father had insisted on minting his son's face onto all the minor currency denominations. The prince found himself instinctively tugging his burlap hood lower over his face.

The captain pulled Janos into a side alley where Legate Avors was casually leaning up against a cracked pillar, carefully observing the bustling crowd.

"Are they still there?" asked Gisele nervously.

"Who?" Janos asked, still feeling a bit jostled.

The captain ignored him, "I wasn't talking to you," she looked up at Legate Avors, "well?"

"It's *Legate*, captain. And yes, they're still there, across the square."

"Who's there?" asked Janos again, feeling his annoyance growing.

The Grey Isle Tale

Gisele also casually peaked around the pillar now, studying the bustling market stands lining either sides of the humble village lane which eventually becomes the great Oskane Way. The road then leads north through the village of Trenae before sweeping away west, skirting the northern edges of Mount Silvertine before angling southwest, down towards the Imperial Seat of the Grey Isle, Senokia. The captain ducked back into the alley and let out a sigh as if she had been holding her breath.

"Scypiasians," she said quietly, as if they could be overheard amidst the murmuring festival and trumpets signaling the parades' readying.

Janos groaned, "how do they know where we are?"

"My Prince... don't be silly... if you can possibly help it," Gisele said, rolling her eyes.

Legate Avors shot her a warning sort of look before continuing to watch the squad of Scypiasian Hastati working their way through the oblivious crowds, hunting for them.

"What, what will you do, legate?" she quipped.

"Are you always this impertinent, captain?" Avors shot back.

"No, this is just something special I reserve for snotty Ulians... sir."

The prince spied the squad nearing. He could see the glint of the Scypiasian's silver-edged spears and short swords – already he could feel his inner darkness itching – as if some painfully persistent rash of poison ivy had inflamed his skin, crawling up and down his arms and chest. Janos coughed loudly, hoping to politely interrupt his spatting companions.

"You ignorant peasant, If you weren't a lady and I weren't a gentleman..."

"*Lady. Gentleman.* Pah - Pretty words – They're just pretty words cowards who treat their own people as second-class citizens use to hide behind, Legate."

The wolf sigil of House Scypiasian was snuffling ominously nearer. The squad crossed the jammed street, packed full of colorful revelers oblivious to the trio's plight. Janos coughed louder this time.

"You forget your place!"

"See this... *this* is my point, exactly," said Captain Gisele as she rolled her eyes exasperatedly.

Part of Janos wanted to just let them keep arguing – bickering and fighting... just like his own royal mother and father had, behind closed palatial doors, once upon a time. The prince shook his head. He suddenly felt tired. Mentally fatigued from the never ending effort it took to keep his other half at bay.

"Um... legate... captain?"

"What!?" they both snapped back at Janos.

The prince only pointed awkwardly. The hunting pack of Scypiasians were nearing the cobblestone alley were the trio had been loitering over-long. If it were not for a providential cart laden heavily with syrupy cordials and sticky-sweet rolls trundling past, the group would have already been discovered.

"Follow me – I have not visited our estates since I was but a boy – but I bet I still remember the side entrance through the stables from here... I hesitate to think of what our entrance would stir if we just barged into the middle of the celebration with our Scypiasian friends now," ushered Avors.

Gisele eyed her verbal sparring partner dangerously as she passed. Janos smirked. Even with his capacity to feel pain now vastly diminished, even he could feel the captain's icy demeanor as he hurried deeper down the alleyway after the legate.

The trio turned away from the wide verandas and arched stone columns of the dark cherry red tiled buildings curled with trumpeter vines and wild grapes for a time-beaten earthen footpath which wound fairly, but not quite straight towards the unmistakable smells and sounds of horses. The way led through an iron gate. At first glance, it appeared to be solidly locked – but with a deft jiggle from the legate – it swung squeakily inwards and onwards. The stalls they passed through were mostly empty – the prize show horses and stallions having already been led out to pull the apple-laden wagons or prepped and pampered for the harvest parade. Each member of the little band felt his or her guard and senses slowly lower as the smell of good earth and farmyard intoxicated their minds and hearts with ease.

Janos was lost in wonder. All this was his? – or would have been by rights. This little baron's stable – small in comparison to the royal stables he was accustomed to back in the capital, Senokia, anyway – but the homeliness... the warmth and familiarity... almost quietly pacified his darker half. The prince could feel his untimely scars slicing his back ache with a longing he had never really felt before. A yearning for a home. Not the palace upbringing, or the physical building in which one was raised... maybe not even the land one hailed from... but something... somewhere... else. Janos's eyes trailed Gisele's soft, tumbling hair bounce along her shoulders as they strove to keep up with the taller commander – intimately more familiar with his surroundings and their way through stable doors and porticos. Every now and again, their guide would give a knowing nod to a stray attendant, busy at their last tasks of the day. Suddenly, the maze ended, spilling Captain Gisele, and Prince Janos out into wheat field ripe as old copper. The field sloped gently up a hill, crowned with an ancient tower wearied with shaggy ivy.

"Oh, lovely – another tower..." groaned the captain, brushing her hair out of her eyes.

"Not just any tower, captain. My tower. The foundations of this estate are founded upon far older ones, they say. And this is the last physical outcropping of them."

"Do you mean to say," asked the prince, "this tower was from that of those first discovered by the grandsons of Longinus the Builder, who founded our very Rumenjian Empire?" he craned his head up the curving, cylindrical fortification.

"Yes, Your Majesty – the very same. Or, at least this is but one poor example remaining of it. My ancestors found the ruin and the orchards – run very much wild by then, of course... but all the same... it is indeed curious to imagine the sorts of people who once lived on our island."

Avors now began feeling around inside the ivy covered wall on the tower's side which faced away from the estate and reveling town.

"I always wanted to know," asked Gisele quietly, suddenly hushed as if in temple, "who were they? The ones who lived here before civilized men came, I mean?"

With a stumble, Avors unlatched some hidden hook and a great arc of ivy swung inwards. "Well, that's the great mystery, isn't it, Brutajian? Considering all the resources, might and power of our grey island can muster... why did these lands' former masters disappear?"

"Something for the scholars to puzzle, I guess?" answered Janos, in hushed tones.

They entered now, gazing up at the old beams, somehow still magically untouched by ages and ages untold – free from the fingers of the North Wind and the bite of cold winter's teeth. The tower was utterly still. The sounds of the festival, up till then a mile or so off but still recognizable, abruptly faded away.

Janos' scars itched. Something silver must be nearby. While his heart felt quietly at peace, the prince could feel his darkness grow anxious and dubious. He suppressed a grimace as best he could. "So what now, legate – we've been brought into sanctuary at last – for I don't doubt this serves as some sort of safe-haven, at any rate."

"Yes," said Avors softly, "it is a sanctuary... or, at least a boy's sanctuary..." he smiled with a distant, lingering gleam in his eyes. "Before life took me away to Senokia... to capital politics and wills higher than mine... ah, the capital... to a life which eventually led me back here, once more... as a stranger, hooded and cloaked in my own ancestral lands."

"What is that!" exclaimed Gisele suddenly. A little to their left, dark, faded writing had been scratched deeply into the stone walls. The language was curving and foreign... indecipherable, yet ominous and foreboding all the same. Underneath the hasty scrawl two symbols could be made out... one of a dark skull, and the other a sort of 'V' shaped symbol etched like a bird in soaring flight, maybe. The writing would have been only curious... but something about the unnatural darkness of the skull's hollow eye sockets raised the hairs on the back of everyone's necks.

"I don't know, captain. But my grandfathers would tell tales from the early days on the islands... you've probably heard of some of them yourself, Prince Janos... tales of how many of the ruins bore old signs of some desperate struggle... scorch marks... siege-dykes... skeletons one or two to a room... sometimes in piles..." Avors shivered, "...used to give me nightmares as a child, though. But never mind all that – up the stairs we go, now."

They trotted up the stairs – each step their boots took felt heavier than the last. Finally, they reached the top of the winding stone stair. The window under the turreted room gave them a wide, commanding view of the country side. Away to the east, Gisele could see the white peak of Mount Silvertine and the river lands which wrapped around its skirting knees shadowed beneath. Towards the west, she could see the milling town, its streets thronging full of life – and beyond, rows and rows of orchards, until the backsides of the rocky sea cliffs began, sheer and daunting. And if Gisele strained, she might just make out the guarding towers and a hint of the glinting, restless sea shining at the edge of the familiar world she knew so well.

"You ought to be safe enough here, my prince... for now, at the very least," said Avors after a moment of savoring his childhood nostalgia.

Janos raised his eyebrows, "going so soon, Avors?"

Avors nodded with a terse smile, "yes Prince Janos... I need to gather information and take stock of the local situation. Unfortunately, it would appear in my absence, another family may have laid claim to Trennin. In happier times, you would be a guest lavished in my humble home! Alas, now the days are sour as wormy apples." He took a step back down the stairs and then poked his head back up, "but we shall see what the night brings. Please make yourself comfortable... I'll bring dinner and supplies as soon as I am able."

Janos nodded and waved a hand, "be careful Avors – Trennin is not as either of us remember, it would seem."

"Of course," Avors agreed. "And you, Brutaejian," he addressed Gisele sternly; "you would do well to remember your place, especially in the presence of your betters." And in a moment he had slipped back down into the soft tower shadows.

Janos looked over at the captain and had to stifle a chuckle. Gisele was heartily pantomiming the legate.

...

Time slowly passed as they waited. The silence of an early autumn evening seemed to grow as day's end slowly waned. As they looked out, they saw the mist creep up along the faded green hills and vales across the land. Down amid the celebrating town, little flickers of orange torchlights began burning one by one as the stars came out above – glittering blue and silver, red and green in the vast heavens above. It was now some time since Avors had first left to gather news. The night closed in all around Gisele and Janos in earnest now, but still they were silent, watching the roll of time transform the countryside all about them. And it seemed, as if they were watching from Heaven itself, the last night of a great empire descended before all faded away to grey dusk.

Gisele eyed Prince Janos' back, where she knew the death scars still lay, silently, like some haunting testimony or some grim prophecy.

Janos felt her eyes on him. In his heart, he wished things had happened differently. He wished this night had never come... that the day which burned brightly only a moment before would have continued forever. But night came for all, eventually. The prince turned to speak, but gasped instead.

"What?" Gisele asked, turning as well.

Looming just beyond Mount Silvertine, the entire sky began to glow orange and red... like an enormous version of the tiny torches below. From horizon to horizon, the whole expanse of the western sky smoldered, for the clouds away there were low and heavy, as they often do when the sea murk rolls in off the Ocean Vaste. Unconsciously, Janos drew near to Gisele, and the captain did not step away.

"Captain, do you know what that is?"

She nodded. Gisele cast her mind's eye back years and years, to when she was little. The night her father had not returned. But the same glow had lit the ocean sky above where the eastern fleet had lay – out for the last exercises of the year before the weather turned. "Dragon. The Sea Dragon."

"He has come at last," said Janos quietly. "It truly is the end, then."

Below them, the little quaint festival carried on, oblivious to the looming threat only a mountain away. There, both the captain and the prince knew Senokia and all the lands along the Ulianskane road burned.

"What do we do now, Janos?" asked Gisele, trying to master her fear. "What can we do?" she added, despairingly.

The prince was quiet for a time, and then said, "we can do what we must."

Presently, heavy footsteps made their way up the spiraling turret steps. Both the pair's hands went to their weapons instantly, but it was only Avors.

"Sire, I've met with friends – all those I could find quickly and quietly during the festival... we..." his gaze flicked to his prince's eyes and then Avors turned and beheld desolation's glow along the western horizon.

"He has come, Avors," said the prince grimly, "and so we must go."

The dozen or so armed men of the legate's house gasped as they eyed the unearthly glow, hazy at the edge of the only world they knew.

"Yes, he has," agreed Avors simply.

Janos nodded as he looked out across the quietly darkening forests and hills. He thought vaguely of the ominous carven words inside the old tower's base. What had happened here on the island once upon a time? The prince shook his head, his mind still wavering slightly at the slowly forming immensity of the task looming up before him. He studied Gisele's curved face, beautiful in the low, glimmering light of the torches and luminous fireflies. Janos saw her freckles and shocks of careless hair tumbling down. He saw the town beyond. The prince thought of the towers, and his now burning home. He remembered the searing pain the assassins' blade had made when it scoured his back. Janos saw in his mind the billowing darkness of something wicked... without form or reason... coming with the crimson flames to burn his world to ashes. Raising a hand, he felt for his medallion. The cool feel of it in the prince's fingers calmed him, somehow.

"I know what we have to do. Listen, all of you. After the attempt on my life, the Scypiasians will not stop. We need the eastern half of the isle, at least, ready to both fight and flee, if the battle goes ill. There is treachery afoot on this day, which may perhaps mark the end of Rumenjia's footing here upon the Grey Isle," Janos took a breath, forcing his mind to steady and strategize, "Avors, I need you to orchestrate the fortification here. Defend the eastern half of the isle as best you can. You need to be ready to both root out the treachery from within and prepare for the dragon's eventual arrival. But you also need to ready every ship you can find in case we must evacuate, too."

Avors face went ashen. "Sire, *are you serious*? Leave the Grey Isle? Where would our people go?"

Janos smiled faintly, the lines across his face became taut and creased, despite his youth, "Go straight east – there the fishing villages lie scattered – you've been there yourself before, when we were younger men. A little beyond them stands what remains of a Rumenjian fort from when times were better. If we have to leave, go there. Bring as many people and supplies as you can, but remember not to tarry – because the dragon will surely not." The prince clasped his friend's shoulder firmly. "Pray we will not have to leave our homes. Take heart and we will see each other again ere the night fades. And it will fade."

"How do you know?" asked one of the legate's frightened men.

"It always does," Janos answered simply.

Avors turned to his group, addressing each in turn. Some would head north to where the roots of the mountain folded down into the great bay and the roads ran straight and broad – and hopefully the northern fleet would still lie anchored. Others would fly south to the southern port where a great many Rumenjians lived along the milder shores. Some would hurry back west and alert the watchtowers – warning against the Scypiasians and telling them to expect trouble. The rest would gather the towns' people. "Go! Gather the loyal for battle – expose those who are in league against us – prepare the rest for the boats. Our country is not our buildings but the people themselves. Think of them, and may their memory speed you upon your way. May the gods go with you."

The legate turned but once more before disappearing into the blackness of night, "Janos... I know what you feel you must do. Please... be... be careful. Know when to fight and when to leave," he set down two bags full of supplies for the prince and the captain gently on the ground.

"Well, that's always the trick, isn't it, my friend," said the prince, the faint starlight glinting like frosty steel in his eyes. "Farewell," and with that, Avors, Legate of the Faithful, disappeared into the night.

"I don't know about any of that... great speeches about whole country or nations... but I do know I'm sticking with you, My Prince. Somebody has to, you know," said Gisele.

"I thought you hated me," Prince Janos replied.

The captain shifted. "I... I don't know what I think or feel," Gisele said, as if she were coming out of a haze. "Nothing matters now, I suppose, except you. I grew up dreaming of meeting you someday... Battles I can handle... but losing people... it's just not something I've ever really been good at," Gisele glanced back out at the fell glow billowing up in the west, "I guess the world's dealt me a bitter hand once more," she sighed, "look, I'm going with you for two reasons. You aren't storming a burning capital to face a dragon so you can avenge yourself, all the while being plagued by assassins who could honestly be anyone on the road all on your own. You just aren't. And... well... the second reason I'm going with you is because..." her bravado flustered away in the true dark and the dancing fireflies.

Janos saw this stubborn Brutajian before him: a soldier, and a compatriot. Gods, he wished he really had met her years ago – had seen the value and use of a woman who was not just passing flash and glitter, lands and dowries... social ranks and all that... but who was brave. For in bravery there is a rarer beauty than all a nation's finery. The darkness in him sneered, unbidden – lashing against its restraints, "she only wants to come along so she can ensure your death when the madness comes. When your death finally finishes the job... and you know it will."

The prince looked down, "you're going to need this," he said finally, handing Gisele a silver knife solemnly.

She took the knife and stowed it away... then, unbidden and hesitant, her smooth hands raised his chin back up, "We will not perish this day. I... I know what you are – or might be. But it isn't really you. I know better. Avors does too, I think." She looked up at him, her eyes lingering on his chin stubble and jawline... up into his shadowed eyes. Gisele thought she could see the darkness itself there – fighting and scratching for control, "I am going for you. Don't forget that, because I mean it word for word."

He nodded sullenly. Janos felt spent inside once more. Inspiring speeches were one thing – grim plans another. With an effort, he lugged his supply pack across his shoulder, as Gisele did the same, "Well... after you then, Lady..."

"It's Perrault... remember?"

"Lady Perrault of house Brutajia of Rumunjia," said Prince Janos softly, bowing formally.

"*Lady*, huh?" Gisele thought, suppressing a deeply satisfying grin in the shadow of the tower they left behind them now... "a girl could get used to the company of princes after all... even if he is Ulian..."

"Well, lead the way my prince," said Gisele finally, "I suppose we can make dinner of whatever meagre fares Legate Bleedy feels suited for both rulers and peasants on the road..."

Before them, the west smoldered – and already, the wind carried the scent of bitter embers blown throughout the Grey Isle before they disappeared across a wine-dark sea.

Chapter III

Fire by Midnight

The duo mounted the pair of horses Avors had left for them near the tower's hidden outlet. Trotting off into the weird semi-darkness felt like watching some nightmarish anti-sunrise. At first they cut across country in order to avoid having to follow the road north through Trennin's sister town, Trenae. Eventually, they hit the Oroskane Way as it curved left towards western lands. This highway became the main road they both knew led to the royal Ulianskane Bridge and then Senokia, the capital of the island. As they traveled, they knew each step took them further into the fiery gloom, each breath closer to the source of the growing fear in their chests.

At times Janos found himself glancing over at Gisele and wondering what she really thought of him. Not that it mattered much now anyways... but still. The already confusing mix of darkness and light within him – the terrible, biting, anxious fear which tore at his stomach now felt a new sensation: excitement. Janos shook his head. He couldn't allow himself to start feeling attracted to Gisele now... of all times. Janos knew his feelings could not go anywhere – not really. Not after his whole life he had been taught just how much people could be different from one another. Not to mention she was only a lowly Brutajian and he was the Imperial Crown Prince of House Ulian.

Sometimes, sparks would cascade down, bright enough under the glowing murk of the hellish skies above to light up her soft cheeks and flowing hair. "Still," Janos thought, "she is a wondrous creature." The prince wished they had met some other way – in some other time and place. "But then again," Janos continued musing, "how else could we have ever met, or been able to see our merits, if not for a time such as this?" The rhetorical question made him feel slightly better. The burning darkness inside him seemed to quake before the nervous enchantment this one simple backwoods captain was casting on him. Janos wondered if Gisele was even aware of what she was doing – how she was making his chest fill up and his head dizzy...

For miles, the prince tried to work up the courage to say something... but the next dusky bend was always a turn too near... the timing always a bit too close for reassurance. They were working through a moonlit vale under the northern skirt of Mount Silvertine now... a ways below their track a river rushed – glittering like rubies and carbuncles in the wan moonlight which at times filtered down through torn shreds of smoky cloud. Janos took a deep breath and felt his amulet rise on his chest. He could now just make out the tinge of sea upon the ashen air, mingled with the pungent aroma of pine forest all around them.

"Cap... Gisele?"

She nodded quietly, as if perhaps she had been eavesdropping on his private internal dialogue for some miles now. "So it's Gisele again, huh, your highness?"

"I..." he wasn't sure how to start. All of Janos' rigorous oratory, speech and rhetoric classes felt utterly useless now... "I... HUSH!"

"Wait... what?" she said, as if startled out of some fair dream she had been waiting for...

"Stop. There are people on the road ahead."

"Well, I can't see any of them," she huffed.

"Well I can... for some reason... never mind that... I think it's best if we get off to the side until they pass us."

Gisele shrugged coolly, trying her best to act indifferent now.

They dismounted and led their steeds off to the right of the road. A little ways within the tall pines, amid the scattered needles, they waited and watched. After what seemed like an agonizing age, a squad of soldiers appeared, leading some poor soul hooded and bound amongst them. The dark night seemed to enfold around them... and Janos cursed their luck... because it meant he could not quite make out the soldier's sigil from his current vantage point.

Presently, Gisele and Janos could make out the soldiers' talk... "it's a good thing we caught this one heading towards what's left of the capital, right centurion?"

One of the other uniformed soldiers nodded grimly, "Quite right, Miles," the centurion gave the prisoner a rough shove and laughed, "and to think old Romestamo here has given us the slip for so long now..."

The squad was coming nearer now... Prince Janos thought he could just make out the prisoners sea-blue robes fluttering in the great in-drafting air now. "Captain..."

"Oh, and now we're back to just regular old captain now, are we? ... Men..." complained Gisele in a whisper.

Janos grinned, and thought hard, "you're not going to like this..."

"It can't be any worse than our special time back in the tunnel now, can it? Seriously, I always seem to pick the guys with the most baggage..."

"Shhhhhhhh."

"Alright, alright. What? You want to rescue the old man or something?"

"That's not just any old man! Yes, I want to free *Romestamo*."

"You WANT TO WHAT?"

"SHHHHHHH."

"IS IT REALLY HIM?? ... BUT IT'S A WHOLE SQUAD!"

Janos struggled to clamp a leather glove over Gisele's overly-noisy mouth. But before they could recover, the duo both saw the troop of soldiers swivel their heads towards the suspicious noise.

"That doesn't sound like an empty pine wood to me..." said Miles.

"We don't have time for this," muttered the centurion, scratching his stubbly chin. "Miles, Immunae – go check it out – and be quick about it. We have to meet up with those creepy Mermen and take Seaport by dawn with this lot or there'll be hell to pay... and we're already running late as it is."

Miles drew his short sword; the blade glinted darkly under the steadily falling embers. Immunae hefted a stout bow and expertly fitted a honed arrow – its triangular head smelled faintly of poison. Together, the two soldiers advanced into the dark woods.

"Centurion – there's a... well it looks like a pair of horses, sir!" called Miles.

"Another one over here, too!" called Immunae in a high, sharp voice, some ways away now.

The centurion rolled his eyes, "and the riders?"

"No one, sir."

"Well, keep looking," the centurion turned now to the rest of his men, "spears out, and stay frosty. There's not supposed to be anyone out on this road tonight... yet."

Suddenly, a lone figure appeared standing in the middle of the road away back towards the direction of Trenae.

"Halt!" cried the centurion.

The mysterious figure began advancing steadily now.

"Imperial business. Be on your way, citizen," the centurion commanded gruffly.

But the figure continued straight for the cluster of soldiers, the order unheeded.

"Last warning!"

The figure now drew a long, silvery blade from his side.

With a sudden flash of recognition, the centurion took a step back. "*You.* You're supposed to be dead!"

"Aren't we all, Brutus?"

"Immunae! Arrow. Now!"

Nothing happened. The figure was drawing nearer and nearer amid the whirling sparks – now close enough for the pallid light to illuminate a grim smirk etched along his young face.

"Immunae!"

"Immunae can't hear you now. I have set his soul free from whatever foul curse your kind has set upon him," a fair voice called out fiercely.

"Damn it. Miles?"

… Nothing.

"Oh – Miles too! Sorry about that…" the same fair, ruthless voice called out from somewhere within the dim pine grove.

The stranger halted a few yards away from the remaining soldiers, who had formed defensively up around their prisoner. "Hello Brutus."

"Your highness," acknowledged the centurion, gripping his long iron spear.

"Where are the rest of your men, Brutus?" Janos said, circling the enemy band now. He could clearly make out a hodgepodge of different house sigils among the three distinct armor styles of the soldiers before him. "So... the conspiracy affects every house, then. I was afraid of that." The prince thought – the traitors before him bore the Bear of House Brutajia, the Wolf of House Scypiasia and the Eagle of his own ruling House Ulian.

"You will meet them shortly, your highness..." the centurion chuckled darkly... "in this life or the next."

The grey death scars on the back of Janos' spine tingled. He could feel his rage growing... his dark side and light side oddly colluding together for once. "I suppose I do owe him a favor returned in kind..." thought Janos idly as he briefly gazed down the sinuous length of his deadly silver sword.

Somewhere high overhead dry lighting crashed – splitting through the smoky mirk like crystalline shards. Still, the prince waited... waited for some unspoken sign. But none came, only more graveyard silence hovering, wraith-like, in the stale, sooty air. Readying his nerves – which still half-screamed warnings of deadly peril – the prince walked calmly towards the armed band with his sword at the ready.

Slice.

Janos took one of the guards' heads off.

"Lancar!" shouted one of the other soldiers in disbelief and disgust. "You'll pay for that!" With a wild but sure thrust, he expertly skewered Janos' side.

Except for a few squirts of blood, nothing happened. Janos laughed and wrenched the spear out of the would-be avenger. The soldier appeared surprised and stunned all at once, "you can thank your centurion for that, soldier," the blood and the wounds began to blossom and flow – but Janos just laughed and laughed... the dark and the light within him wove seamlessly together... into some hellish juggernaut who knew no pain or fear.

Indeed, he had left his compulsion to emotions far behind during the night he had been assassinated by Brutus... after the royal ball, while Janos had been alone, up in his room gazing out wonderingly at the lights and glittering decorations. The prince remembered all the shimmering yellow lights – a royal bedazzlement of the courtyard decked out in all its imperial finery. He had remembered the surprising feel of the knife slicing home as one of his own guards attending him severed his spine once... twice... three times... Janos had lost count after seven. Darkness swarmed over him similar to this sable night, too. But after the assailant fled – his grisly mission an apparent success... Janos opened his eyes. The pain had been unbearable until consciousness finally left him, lifeless in a pool of his own blood which stained through the exquisite rug and seeped across the tiled marble floor before congealing.

It was over. He had died. But... his eyes were still open.

He blinked.

Slowly, Janos remembered turning his head and discovering how it just continued turning... too far... He wasn't sure what to think. Numbly, he had just gotten up – a tricky task amid his own slick lifeblood – while also steadying his head upon his shoulders. Finding a wash basin and a mirror, Janos started cleaning himself up. The prince remembered not thinking... not even once. It had been like muscle memory. As if another life somewhere far which he had read about – memorized... a part in a play he had performed masterfully. After cleaning himself up and changing he had called the servants to come clean up the mess. Janos recalled their looks of utter horror and confusion at the task of cleaning up so much blood.

The prince remembered laughing about it... something about it all just made his body chuckle and grin of its own accord... And it was then, when cold terror had really set in. It was like the feeling of helplessly drowning – something he had almost accomplished once as a young child while carelessly swimming in one of the many waterfall-fed pools among the western edges of the Silvertine. But not it was different – for it was no mossy pool he found himself perpetually drowning in... it was himself. While Janos was in his body, he was powerless... or at least felt that way. Meanwhile, some other... thing... bid his arms wave the servants away after they had more or less finished mopping up his mess. Then some other man stretched and settled his spine back into place with horrific casualness. Janos had tried to scream and found he could not. Janos tried to prevent himself from going back towards the balcony... back to where he... he had died! but could not. He wanted to run... Janos wanted to find his mother and father... He wanted to hide and cover himself... but could not. The prince felt himself waving back down below at his assailant, who was now winking roguishly and waving back up at him with a chillingly knowing grin. Janos was forced to watch as Brutus swung up onto a horse and, instead of rightly fleeing the scene of his own prince's grisly murder; instead, canter by an upright cask of wine. Compelled, he gazed on as the man – if man he was – idly fill a hip flask with the sparkling red liquid... and then ride his horse slowly away, taking care to avoid the last of the ball's revelers who were just then leaving in their own carriages and litters.

Hazily, Janos felt himself phase out of memories and back into the fight at hand. Every ounce of helplessness the flailing Janos remembered being powerless to affect then upon his own limbs that fateful night, he now used to hack into the enemy squad with – utterly careless of wounds he received. Ferocity blurred his vision with murky crimson currents. He took comfort in the amulet anchored securely around his neck, at times now bouncing against his skin – sticky with sweaty physical exertion born from fighting multiple, fairly well-trained opponents.

The prince felt himself slipping back into his memories once more... He remembered how it wasn't until the next day after he had been murdered... after hours of feigned sleep... agonizing hour after hour trapped within his own run-away body, counting chimes from the great clock, until dawn finally came. It was then, as the new day's first wan ray of light filtered across his own stained marble floor, that Janos became shockingly aware of one minute fact: he could still feel one thing. It was only one thing, but it was something. The sudden revelation should have made him gasp... but his body only squirmed uncomfortably. Janos remembered being able to feel the tiniest weighted pull from his ceremonial amulet tugging innocently along his bruised neck. What would have normally irritated him... how the chain of the amulet typically caught and pinched the hairs where his shoulders and neck joined... now felt like the touch of the gods. His body thrashed now... but Janos didn't care. He took the full effect of the feel from the chain pulling his hairs and skin in. The mild pain had become his very life.

He remembered how slowly, his ability to feel spread just a little more. Janos' body tried to hold its breath – a rhythm now wholly unnecessary, yet still familiar... and needed if the illusion of life was to be maintained. Janos blinked his own eyes. Somehow he had known this fact. Never mind how he had known it now... Hey! He had blinked again! Relief and the rising feel of power encouraged him now. Janos felt his determination resolving steadily. This was his body and the prince had never much been one for sharing anyways... being the only son of the Emperor and Empress of the Grey Isle.

Janos recalled the next week; and how the time spent had felt like an entire decade campaigning through foreign territory – everything from systematically identifying his new, strange foes' strengths and weaknesses to halting the enemy's supply lines bolstered Janos' own morale. At first, the prince had avoided open contests of will between their two invisible armies. Janos knew better than to set both host upon each other. Instead, he spent his time securing strategic geographic locations... albeit within his own body and senses... but the game worked. Janos soon learned he was the superior legate.... And the-whatever-it-was... evil spirit? Had also learned... learned to likewise fear its host and second-guess itself. After that moment, each stroke Janos took brought him closer to complete re-mastery.

Like in chess, where each piece had to be taken just so in order for him to achieve his ultimate objective... indeed, it was a struggle Janos was still seeing through to the bitter end. Finally, only scattered insurgents remained of a once vast black army arrayed within him. Mostly, his inner darkness struck now with melancholy moods, and at worst despair... which threatened the prince's typically objective perception of reality. Janos remembered when the final real break-through had come, though. The change came after he finally decided to confide in the only man he felt he could really trust... and so, after a month of carefully calculated thought, he summoned Legate Avors – one of his childhood friends and closest councilor... the older man had been like a father to Janos while his own had been too busy for the boy. Together, over the next decade, they had uncovered and fought through a sinister trail of shadowy intrigue which they soon discovered threatened their entire nation. The undead could be anyone – lurking anywhere at any time. Besides the other, who could they truly trust? There was a conspiracy among their island, and they must be the ones to root it out, or utterly perish in the attempt.

So now Prince Janos was here in the dead of night traveling lonely backroads. With near impunity, he hacked and slashed his way through eight... nine... ten conspirators. Before Janos had engaged the group, he had strained his vision, trying to make out the tint of the soldier's eyes. He had learned how the evil spirit revealed its strength and level of bodily control by the level of darkness shown in its hosts' eyes. Where usually the spark of life glittered brightly with a sacred flame... instead the dull twin inky pools of a demon who is dreaming could glare defiantly back through. These men were all infected. All damned. Their spirits inside, Janos knew, begged for relief... He had a duty to banish these creatures of evil back down to the very pit of Tartarus from whence they came – and silver could do just that.

During his own long bodily campaign, Janos had been delighted to discover his body's newfound revulsion for all things silver... evening meals had never been so enjoyable. Janos' etiquette teacher, who up until recently then had all but given up on him, had instead found a new student, rapt with deadly serious attention over his every word (especially when it came to which fork went where). This, coupled with his unique amulet... an ancient heirloom handed down from father to son all the way back to the Rumenjian founding of his island empire, now served as both his sword and internal shield in his continuing war against the undead.

Before the prince now... only three enemies remained – and one of them was struggling to keep his prisoner contained. Suddenly, flying out of the gloom whistled a familiar silvery knife. With a deadly grace, it sunk home – right into the guard's throat.

"Good for Gisele!" Janos thought with a grin.

The prince was about to work on finishing the final two soldiers off... the work had been relatively easy up till now – especially since the squad was only equipped with regular weapons, unfit for fighting... special contestants like Janos. But a sudden flash of searing blue knocked everyone back.

The wizard had found his staff.

Out of the dazzling azul mist, a booming voice cried with a fury which made even Janos stop dead. Romestamo had been unleashed. The mist, thick as ever – even for the northern part of the Grey Isle – pooled and swirled like long, tangible curtains, shrouding Janos's sight. Again and again he felt his limbs wield his silvery sword, which he had managed to hold onto, slice and hack with experienced precision. He felt as if he were not swinging an instrument of war but of art. Janos was conducting a grand orchestra and here was his baton. The phantom musicians took their places, seated before a packed audience of a magnificently shining concert hall. All the patrons wore masques like, vivid living faces – reactive and eerily expressive. Purple grins and green-rimmed eyes gazed back down at the prince; all the while he conducted his musical triumph before a vast array of faceless players. The masques of the audience called along with the elation of the rising score – voices which began blurrily faded and gradually became sharper, piercing and more distinct with each passing bar of melody conducted... A blue mist was filtering in – opalescent and imperious now...

A tall man draped in sea-blue robes stood before him now. His grey-white hair drooped down to his shoulders; and a matching beard pricked out like a thorn from underneath his deep, shadowy hood. At first Janos wondered if the man was another audience member... until he saw the stranger's glittering eyes – full of starlight and the color the sky takes just before an eastern sunrise.

"Stop," – the man had never moved his mouth, but the words had come from everywhere at once.

"Janos, stop."

But the chorus of the music was rising, soaring higher and higher into unearthly regions of passion now... dare the prince stop? Janos' vision shifted. The blue mist faded into clearer white and he saw... were they soldiers? Fallen soldiers all around him – hacked and hewed lying scattered all around... with the dizzying sense of a great distance between himself and his body, the prince slowly looked down at his hand which gripped a decorated silver sword covered in red blood glinting under the night sky.

"Janos, you can stop now. Come back. Come back from out of deep water and the abyss' edge."

With a rush which made no noise and took no time, Janos felt himself once again fully aware and in control of his faculties. Bile rose up in his tightening throat as he observed all the carnage surrounding him. How could someone do this to other people? Had... he done this? The rising horror filled him with revulsion. Staggering away from the circle of death, Prince Janos stumbled into the tall grass and weeds which grew haggardly up next to the roadside. He could feel himself rapidly breathing short breaths as his body's reflexes attempted to dry heave. Dropping his dirty weapon, Janos grabbed his knees, shaking.

Suddenly, a hand tenderly touched his shoulder and then timidly floated over to where his death-wounds peppered his back just below his neck. The prince could feel the soft hand hover for a moment, and then gently console him. Janos closed his eyes and exhaled. Hot tears rimmed his red eyes. He was babbling now... babbling on and on like an eternally rushing stream... about that night he had been murdered. About what he had to do... about what no one should ever have had to face alone... in the dark.

Finally, Janos wiped his face and cleared his sodden vision, and turned to face his comforter. Vaguely, he had imagined it was Romestamo standing behind him... but it wasn't. It was Gisele. She stood there like some angel from heaven... like a living Mercy or winged Nike enfleshed. Her expression was timeless. Somewhere in her deep brown eyes, infinite sorrow, fear and pity mingled. With complete disregard for all the cultural rank and pomp he had been schooled in all his life – with intentional abandonment of prejudice and social aversion – without fear or reason – Janos embraced her passionately. At first, he just clung desperately to Gisele like a drowning man clings for a lifeline tossed into a sable maelstrom. Janos wasn't aware for how long he hugged her, as if all the safety and love in the world had coalesced into the living, visible form of one single woman: Captain Gisele Perrault.

Like waking abruptly from dreams, Prince Janos felt himself eventually pull away from her open embrace. Inside, he could feel the old internal walls of decorum rising back up again... but now the prince was sure the once locked and barred gates of iron stood open. It was an odd feeling. Janos' chest felt like he had breathed gales of fresh, clear springtime – like buttery yellow sunlight had lit up what once had been ancient, rotting dungeons filled with moldering decay. Janos felt the corners of his lips tug into a timidly gentle smile... but he felt too embarrassed to make eye contact just yet.

"Hi," was all the prince could manage.

The captain was silent for a moment... her eyes full of some inexpressible emotion. "Hello," she softly replied.

For a brief moment they beheld each other, both unsure of what to say next. The sound of two heavy feet plodding steadily towards them, accompanied by the patient wooden knock of a long, sturdy walking stick approached them. The prince and the captain turned to meet the newcomer – it was Romestamo, of course.

The older man stood before them now, his face had only just begun to take on a distinctively wizened look, but it was his eyes which spoke volumes. This man, if man he was, had been through the darkest darkness and had impossibly come out the other end more or less intact. Romestamo's frame was tough and lean like a hound. His long sea-blue cloak encompassed his whole frame like a rolling wave frozen in mid crash. Janos watched as Romestamo studied him intently. The prince decided the famed wizard's presence was a touch imposing – and besides, Janos wasn't sure how he felt being thoroughly read like an open scroll. After one final brief glance towards Gisele, which came and went as swiftly as a sure-footed traveler reading a road sign, Romestamo the Wizard relaxed ever so slightly and appeared to be waiting for them.

Gisele was cold. The adrenaline it had taken to ambush those two... she would have said soldiers, but she knew better by the dead look in their eyes... had all but worn off now. She could just now feel her hammering heart beginning to calm back down to its regular steady rhythm. But the sweat on her skin from all the exertion chilled her to the bone. She shivered. The feeling of the prince, so close to her chest, still lingered in her mind. After he had collapsed into her embrace Gisele hadn't thought – just reacted. Part of her remembered singing her younger sister to sleep during stormy winter nights in their home by the sea... Sometimes, years later, when the wind had howled through the crannies of Tower Oros, she could still remember the smell of Daniele's auburn hair as she fell asleep, finally comforted. But the prince... he was different. He was a man who had seen and even been an unspeakable horror. Janos. Prince Janos... saying his name in her mind had only just now revealed a hint of some intoxicating exoticness. But what he had unleashed on all those things masquerading as soldiers scared, even terrified Gisele, too.

"I mean, I am glad we rescued Romestamo, aren't I?" she mused. "But on the other hand…" Gisele sighed and tried to focus on the newest twist in her adventure which had already taken her far from home. Romestamo the Wizard was now so near she could but have taken a trifling few paces and touched him. The man was a legend. He had been a part of the stories Gisele had heard all her life growing up along the eastern coastlands of the Grey Isle. His tale wove in and out of all the local stories – some so grandiose she was almost sure they were blatant lies – to others which seemed almost laughably common place. The wizened old man with the sea-blue robes and the magic walking stick… a character from some other far-distant tale only hinted at, now living and breathing before her very eyes. The captain did a little half curtsy… it just wasn't the same without a nice flowing dress… but the gesture was simple and well meant, even still.

Romestamo returned the kindness with an easy bow, dipping slightly lower than Gisele had bended, and smiled a warm, honest sort of smile. His face was transformed momentarily – like the rising of the sun spreading wrinkles all across the lines upon his cheeks and near his eyes.

"Oh, his eyes…" thought Gisele, "they look as if they remember something so good and far away…" she blushed a little, thankful that the darkness hid her mild embarrassment of actually curtsying like a little country girl politely greeting some friend of father's… the action had been so childish… but part of her felt somehow safer in Romestamo's silent company.

"Well," said Janos, emotion still obviously shaking his voice just a little, "are we ready to continue, then?"

The captain nodded, but still remained where she was. For a moment longer, Gisele waited for Romestamo to reply… but then gave a quiet laugh, "oh, I forgot! You really aren't the talking type, are you?" she said to the wizard.

Romestamo only smiled and nodded patiently.

"Well, in that case you and I better see if we can get our horses back, Janos," said Gisele.

"Right," the prince agreed.

After a little bit of searching they found both their steeds not far from where they had left them… still standing quiet-eyed in the pine woods. After a moment, the trio continued down the dark road… and slowly, with each deliberate clip and clop, they left the grisly hoodwinks were they lay far behind them. The going was slower now, for the wizard had no horse. But Romestamo made no audible complaint – only quickened his long, easy pace. Gisele had some growing suspicion he knew more than he let on, though.

"Who just follows two random people down a dark road into certain death, with a dragon likely waiting at the end, while the ashes of our capital waft down on us, anyways?" thought Gisele. But it only took one look at the Wizard to know the answer. The older man caught her gaze and nodded… then looked back at her as if to reply, "You do, too."

Gisele looked up to check on Janos. He was a little ways ahead now, continuing to plod along while scanning the ash-ridden road for any more company they might encounter. "Can you… hear me?" the captain quietly asked Romestamo.

His eyes twinkled underneath his cowl-like hood.

Making a mock gasp, the captain smirked and shook her head.

The older man only shrugged and kept walking.

Chapter IV

Grey Dawn

The trio had eventually stopped to rest sometime deep into the night. Morning eventually dawned somehow, impossible and sudden like some glimmering jewel. But what the first rays revealed was not pleasant. Smoke lurked in the dells of the western skirts of Mount Silvertine. At first, one might have mistaken the sooty clouds for tranquil mist or fog, which usually lingered early on in the day. On particularly spectacular autumn mornings, the mist would lap the mountainsides like ocean along the seashore. Blues and silvers would reflect off the immaculate snowy crag of the iconic landmark's snowline. Birdsong and gull's cries would sing in the tree hollows while the faint, ever-present tang of the sea would season the air, pungent and refreshing.

But today was not one of those mornings. Janos had still been afraid to sleep. He was pretty sure the darkness within knew this, too. Whenever he did dream, it was always of blood and destruction... but every once in a great while – Janos would remember phantastic visions he had never witnessed before. Where they former memories of previous hosts? He could never quite tell... But once, just once, the prince had remembered with a tangibly bitter, painful longing which did not belong to him, images of piercing white light and endless rolling green fields. In the distance stood impossibly tall mountains, golden and purple with their own inner light, and beyond Janos somehow intuitively knew, lay The City. But whatever this even meant, he had never been able to puzzle out. With an involuntarily shock and shudder, Janos was wretched away from the keyhole of his own mind, like some naughty, uncomprehending child caught eavesdropping. That night he dreamed of an infernal abyss – Tartarus most likely. Always, in this dream, there was a kind man dressed in white whispering something which obviously ought to have been comforting... but always the darkness within Janos tried at first to ignore and then noisily screech and wail just to drown out the man's compassionate words...

"Janos."

The prince felt himself thrash in his uneasy sleep.

Purple-blue mist floated into his dream's vision – completely out of place with the usual sequence of scenes and acts.

"These are not your dreams, Janos. Awake now."

"MMMM...."

"Janos. Hey, Your Highness... wake up!" Someone shoved him.

Janos jolted awake. The transition from someone else' dreams to full waking felt worse than a bucket of ice water his etiquette teacher had once used on him after he had fallen asleep during a particularly dry lesson. "I'm up... I'm up." The prince grumbled, bear-like.

"Hey Mr. Wizard – I finally got him to wake up." Grinned Gisele... "I swear," she said, turning back to Janos, "you sleep like the dea..." The captain turned ashen and then suddenly found something immersive and intriguing about her pack's brass strap buckle.

Prince Janos clenched his jaw and grimaced, "its fine," he lied. Getting up gingerly, he stretched, carefully noting where the previous night's violent encounter had loosed his body's internal stitching. Janos sighed. He wondered how much more of this existence he could endure. He caught Gisele's hesitant little smile – and then all the lurid sunshine filtering down through the crimson ash lost all remnant of its dire warning. He felt himself smile back. Janos marveled at just how unused to sheepishly grinning his facial muscles were, acting out this simple movement.

"But it feels good," Janos reflected, re-buckling his ornamental sword belt.

...

The morning sun, feeble though it was, eventually cut through most of the somber red mist, revealing the long Ulianskane road the trio had been following ever since their encounter with the undead patrol the previous night. Below them could only be described as freshly sown devastation, utter and complete. Beyond, their road arched over a long bridge and causeway which spanned Lake Rey, leading into whatever was left of Senokia. Even from their great distance, Gisele could see the desolate towers of their once great capital – which had recently been so full of life, now appear utterly empty. Only fires flickered here and there – their great flames licking the heavens in unhindered greed. The smoke from the ruinous citadel floated up and away into the bright autumn skies like a solemn votive offering.

Gisele felt quiet. Hushed like the first time she had visited one of the great temples of her people.

"How?" This one, single word echoed again and again in her head.

She had to purposefully stop her arms from clutching her gut. The crowning jewel of her island people, along with so many innocents had been annihilated overnight. The loss was tangible. Something... innumerable somethings had been taken from her... just like that. Gisele couldn't take her eyes away. Numbly, the captain felt her eyes trying to trace the way she had taken into the city the night of the royal ball. The movement felt like muscle memory. But so far into the once fair streets, which crisscrossed like a spinner's weave until finally coalescing into a single main artery which, Gisele knew, would arrive at the palace gates, was gone. Obliterated and lost amid the black-smoldering wreckage. The captain eventually wrenched her gaze away from the wondering horror of their imperial capital over to the prince. He was so still. Like the dead. Like the dead... but every now and again

Janos would blink, and Gisele would breathe another sigh of relief. Next, she turned and watched Romestamo.

The wizard stood stock still, too – leaning heavily on his staff. His eyes seemed at once both far away and very near. But the older man's expression was like that of a priest's at a great funeral. Sad, stately, solemn and utterly, almost painfully, respectful... as if what and how he officiated meant the fixation of countless mourners' memory of this one, significant moment. Suddenly, he raised an arm and pointed... both Gisele and Janos followed his straining finger to the only large tower clearly remaining in the palace grounds. Tiny little flashes of light flickered now and again... and then they all saw it: a singularly massive shape, clear as the darkest cloud against the pale flickering white castle stones. It was huge – monstrous. With vast, hurricane-strength wings outstretched like a tattered storm on the horizon... the kind which flares up with sudden, unpredictable violence which sailors fear the most. Its scales were glittering razors, sable in the morning sun which it seemed to mock with its very existence. The tail went and went and went... on and on... wantonly smashing remaining stonework like dry kindling, spitefully ignorant of its own sacrilege.

They had gazed upon the Sea Dragon at last.

...

Walking through the dead town was eerie, to say the least. Janos had seen razed towns before... but this. The Imperial city... violated like this... it was beyond his imaginative scope. Trudging past yawning, crooked doorways which led down and away into hell unnerved him... and excited his own inner darkness. The prince felt as if all the newly formed ghosts gawked at him and his companions as they passed by... specters gaunt and already terribly hungry and piercingly cold. In Janos' mind's eye, he tried to remember how the city had been just a few weeks before... The arching gateway had been cast down, scorched and powered into gravel. To the right there had stood his favorite café, The Green Siren. If the prince closed his eyes, he could still hear the horses trotting proudly in – the market's babbling cry – just around the corner, the best smithy in the city, Dwarven Heart Forge, had once filled an entire block with the ring of raining blows glancing off prized armor, weapons and jewels... now empty. The prince felt, at times, like a child tottering from one pile of glowing ashen ruin to another... as the trio slowly made their way through the wreckage as best they could.

Their labor was sluggish. What once would have taken Prince Janos perhaps only twenty or thirty minutes on horseback with a crier clearing the streets before him now took the trio an agonizingly slow snails' pace. Where once they could have shot straight along the expertly laid streets, running like speeding arrows exactly along the four cardinal directions Janos, Gisele and Romestamo now had to wend their way, zigzagging through tottering alleys or past collapsed building still burning. The silence, only interrupted by crackling house fires which at first seemed so uncanny soon became commonplace, until one barely noticed it anymore. This is why they may be excused, perhaps a little, for what happened next...

Chapter V

The Dead Speak

Janos, who had been trying his best to ignore all the unseemly whispering from the newly departed spirits, was slowly becoming separated from the Wizard and Captain Gisele. After a turn or two through the broken streets, he realized he was alone. Panting from scrambling over ruins, Janos lost his balance and tumbled down a small jagged pile of jumbled masonry... the sun shot out through the mirk for a moment... and there before him was a ghostly figure... pale and wan in the golden sun.

"Rachele?"

"Janos? Janos!" her voice came feebly... as if over an impossibly far distance. She continued to search for Janos, as if the few feet now between them were equally as far... some vast space over a stormy sea.

"What are you still doing here?" the question tumbled out of the prince's mouth.

"Janos....? I can barely hear or see you... but... I'm so cold. I... would you...?"

The prince nodded – he remembered his literature lessons well enough. Spying a withered elder tree, ragged and half split in the courtyard's center; Janos trotted over and plucked up one of its broken splinters. Returning, he used the sharp stick to cut a small line in his arm. A small, angry crimson trickle of blood dripped down into a cranny in the shattered street near the ghost's feet.

"W...would you mind?" Rachele asked, a bit sheepishly.

"Oh... sure," said Janos, and turned his back. The prince kept his elder wand at the ready – if he was remembering the old tales right... ah yes... here came crowding all the nearby ghosts now.

"Back! BACK! It is not for you!" Janos cried, brandishing his wooden stick. Most of the ghostly figures retreated a few paces... their pale eyes betrayed their pitiable yearning. A dozen or so began attempting to advance menacingly from different angles. Janos drew his silver sword now, too.

"It is enough," said a quiet voice beside him, as a ghostly hand appeared to alight on his shoulder.

Janos turned to see Rachele wipe the last of the blood from her mouth. "Janos," she called his name again, now stronger. The sun went behind the dull mirk once more and her form could have almost passed for a living person's now.

"Rachele, what are you doing here...?" Janos asked, his voice lowered into a dull hush. The pale, ever so slightly translucent face stared sadly back up into his.

"Oh Janos, how I've missed you," came the calling girl, wispy and faint in the stale, dead air.

"I know... dear sister. I know."

She slowly circled him, eyeing him up and down. "The sickness came for me before your royal ball – remember?" Rachele's spirit said as if she were reminding herself. She seemed so nonchalant... like some forgotten springtime flower, dried and tucked away inside a book never to be opened again.

"I... I remember. Mother and Father were heart-broken... they tried every physician in the land..."

She smiled a little. "I know... they're here with me now, too. We miss you, Janos."

Janos didn't know what to say, so he sheathed his sword and looked into his departed sister's face. All along, he had known it was highly probable that his mother and father had been taken by the dragon... but he had pushed this miserable thought as far down and away as possible. Now, in the moment of truth, Janos didn't really know how to react.

"What is it like?" he finally asked.

She laughed, "oh... dear, sweet Janos... you always were so afraid... I... I'd almost forgotten. It's nothing. Nothing. That's what makes it so funny... so many people... so afraid of death they forget how to live. Really!" she said after Janos gave her a confused sort of look. "Less than a thought – easier than blinking... though... the split moment before is terrifying. One moment you feel completely out of control... now that is a bit scary. I was coughing and coughing... and then I wasn't."

Janos looked up and away for a moment, wishing the sun far away would peek out again and warm his shivering skin. His eyes caught the cracked towers of his former home... flickering with blasts of flame... shuddering now and again. The prince squared his shoulders. He remembered now what he had to attempt. "Rachele... I..."

But a ghostly finger quieted him, "we know, little brother... and understand that if you really do decide to face him, we will be there too..."

Janos nodded glumly, "sometimes... sometimes I wish I could just join you now, you know."

Rachele only smiled benignly, "your time is not yet..." but she paused here... her eyes widened and she drew back.

Now it was Janos' turn to smile sadly. He had wondered how long it would take her to see his shadow inside... "It happened right after the ball," the prince explained. He could see Rachele struggling to understand, half hidden behind a leaning marble pillar. Janos gingerly lifted the medallion up and showed it to the ghost.

She cocked her head and drifted hesitantly closer. "Your necklace?" she said, wonder and doubt mixed in equal measure now, "how?"

Janos shook his head, "I don't really know, exactly... but I'm not going to argue with results, either."

Rachele frowned, "you frighten me... little brother."

"Even as a spirit, you mean I can still scare you?" Janos giggled softly.

"Stop it! This isn't funny."

"What are you going to do... tell mom and da...?" Janos started to say. The brief absurdity of the situation hurtled back to reality.

"... Only if you want me to, Janie."

The prince nodded. He could feel his grin slipping from his face now. "Why aren't you across the River? We gave you the coins and everything..."

Rachele floated over to a nearby rubble pile and did her best to imitate a sitting motion. "I know you did... and I'm grateful. But a funny thing happened on the way... I... well... I was waiting by a river bank... along Styx, I think... there... there were many others waiting too. But a man tapped me on the shoulder... I would have jumped with surprise (you know how I am... or was), but this man with a kind face called my name. Oh, the sound of his voice... it was like I had never really heard the sound of my own name called until that moment. It was strange... I looked out and somehow... I don't know... I could tell he was calling all of our names... calling and calling, if only we'd listen..."

"Did you recognize him?" Janos asked.

Rachele hesitated, "I... well I don't know exactly. But he seemed familiar all the same... like we'd known each other from far away and long ago… but he told me I could go home whenever I wanted…but…"

"But what?"

"Well, the way he said home was like how he had spoken my name. He said home and I felt in my heart like it really was Home… and now it was as if the castle and the Grey Island were only a passing fancy…but never mind that… the man could tell I was a bit hesitant, so he asked if I wanted to do anything before I went on with him."

"What did you want to still do, then?"

"Isn't it obvious, Jan?"

Janos shook his head.

"You never were very bright…. Oh Janos… I just wanted to see everyone again…one more time. But when I came back just now… it was all… this," she swept a ghostly arm around at all the desolation surrounding them.

"You're telling me," Janos sighed.

"I think I was allowed to visit so I could try and help you, little brother."

"How?"

"I'm not sure yet. But I'll be with you until the end."

"Till the end…" Janos murmured.

"Go… get on… you have a dragon to slay. What did you think all those days skipping out on etiquette lessons to play knight in the fields were for, anyways?"

The prince laughed painfully, then took a deep breath and surveyed the burning city. His eyes first went up to the flickering castle… but then back down to rest upon the guiding spirit of his lost sister, "can I really do it, defeat *the* sea serpent?"

"The man never told me. But I suppose that what we're all here to find out now. Go on... your friends need you... they are about a mile or so west of here," Rachele's shimmering form told him.

"Rachele?" the prince called out to the quickly fading form.

"Yes?" called the spirit, nearly invisible now.

"I miss you too. I love you."

The wind skittered cinders and torched leaves across the empty courtyard, leaving nothing but a painful longing.

Janos' gaze still lingered over the pile of stone where Rachele's spirit had last been. The prince turned west, towards his friends – towards the dragon and the feeble afternoon sun, and set off.

Chapter VI

Old Friends

Meanwhile, Romestamo and Gisele continued stumbling through cosmopolitan carnage... the terrain swiftly became grimmer with each passing step taken. And the mood was not relegated to only the scenery either. Gisele especially felt her heart and mind gradually darken and numb... drug-like. Strange thoughts bubbled up from within her own mind... like half-formed creatures she knew not where they came from. Gisele was just about to clamber up and over a prostrate marble pillar when Romestamo's arm shot out, holding her back. She gasped and jumped – almost losing her own balance on the precarious rubble pile they were standing on. The captain looked over at him. She could not see his face, now shrouded in his own deep, sea-blue cowl. But he held up a single quieting finger, urging Gisele to silence. In the split second of a moment, the captain thought she could make out the starry glint of the wizard's eyes... like the heavenly sparkle of stars across a foamy ocean on a calm august night. Gisele blinked and sighed. Relief swept up and washed away her melancholy like a cleansing tide.

Before them was a clearing, and across its once spacious distance the cracked gates of the Ulian citadel now sagged, one of the banners still shamefully smoldered, draped across the threshold. But it wasn't the shocking view of their desecrated capital's seat of royal power which held their gaze... Even without Romestamo's telltale pointing, Gisele could clearly see several units of soldiers, each baring mixed house sigils guarding the castle, ignorant of the charred wreckage all about them.

Hope flared up in the captain's heart. Perhaps there were survivors after all! But the blue wizard shook his head sadly and quietly continued to thrust a knarled finger... Gisele strained her eyes, trying to study whatever hallmark sign

Romestamo saw. Yet before she could figure it out, a cry came suddenly from the left, followed by a hail of silver arrows. The units of guards, momentarily stunned, whirled towards their right, attempting to engage their hidden attackers... when a charge came from the other direction. Even Gisele could make out the charging soldiers now... each of their wide body-shields clearly carried the emblazoned white wolf sigil of House Scypiasia. Pinned between peppering blasts of archer-fire and a professionally formed spear and shield wall, the guards were quickly becoming overwhelmed. Scypiasian victory appeared assured until something massive shook the ground from away inside the citadel grounds beyond the gate. The tremor was so severe, one of the teetering gatehouse walls crumbled like wet sand. All the figures striving in the yard stopped in mid-action. Gisele and Romestamo looked at each other with wide, searching eyes... and in a fraction of a second, the captain realized the prince was missing.

Janos was gone!

But before she could attempt mentally retracing their steps or even began helplessly worrying about him, a piercingly cold darkness erupted up through the gaping holes in the castle walls and yawning gate. As a small girl, Gisele had often accompanied her father out on deep-sea fishing excursions on their boat, the Fair Face... once, during the last run of the year in mid-November, during a squall, she had been knocked over-board into the icy, watery depths. Down and down... she had suddenly plunged... Her body swiftly lost feeling as she tried to gasp and struggle, panicking. The last thing Gisele had remembered was staring down into the abyss, idly wondering if it would be her grave. The next thing she knew she was retching up sea-water... her throat burned and the whole crew was gathered around her, staring. Her father's stricken face peered down into her own. To this day, the warmest thing Gisele could remember were his tears splashing down onto her cheeks as he held her tight, utterly relieved.

But this freezing, billowing storm of darkness went far beyond the terror she had felt the day she had nearly drowned. If it hadn't been for the simple warmth from Romestamo's hand clutching hers as they hunkered down behind the marble column, Gisele would have lost sense of all direction and orientation. If not for the soft, blue glow of his cloak, eyes and staff-tip – now only just visible when it was darkest – she would have, in pure terror, laid down and wished for death. Out of the sweeping, unnatural night laughter drifted... presumably from the remaining undead guards. Indistinct orders were being called from either side of the clearing below them. Gisele imagined the Scypiasian commanders were trying to regroup their divided forces against this new threat. It was what she would have tried to do in their position...

Suddenly, both the wizard and the captain felt the lurking immensity of some massive malevolence upon them. It was as if that uncanny fear of deep water had come, now enfleshed, rising up from the depths to take them. Gisele's heart pounded like a forge-hammer, but she forced herself to remain hidden and gripped Romestamo's leathery hand all the tighter. It was in this small, helpless moment that Gisele realized just how much sheer power Romestamo himself carried, wrapped under his old tattered cloak. Even in the face of utter billowing oblivion just over the jagged rise, his serene calm was like an abiding mountain, patient and steady.

"Who is he?" she thought. The last remaining ray of light slipped behind a veil, as if its innocence could not bear to watch the atrocious acts continue unfolding any longer. Gisele was boggled by how the overwhelming darkness and cold barely even fazed the wizard. Even still, it took another few moments for the captain to realize Romestamo wasn't really actually hiding, either... more like... was he waiting?

Something massive shook the remaining citadel walls. From where the pair crouched, they could hear the ear-splitting sound of the remaining masonry crumble into dust. The dim sounds of soldiers – whether Scypiasian or otherwise was fading obscurely into a dead, thick darkness now so tangible the only thing Gisele could clearly even see was the soft, blue glow of Romestamo. It seemed to her now that the darker and more terrifying the world outside became, the more she appreciated the faint, luminous light emanating from her mysterious companion. There was something almost hypnotically beautiful about the million shades of blue humming next to her.

Romestamo was dreaming again. The darkness always reminded him of the light of his home, far away across oceans and realms. He had been chosen for a hard task. This was his dark road to travel, but not alone... the wizard missed his traveling companion. But they had become separated some time ago, and now it was his task alone to bring light to dark places. Romestamo looked down at the scared child huddled near him... Captain Gisele looked utterly terrified. He had watched so many precious faces go small and dark with fear and passing shadow. The wizard couldn't help himself but laugh, just a little... and out piercing through the blasting, billowing cold emanating from the sea serpent, his deep blue eyes twinkled. Briefly, he put a comforting hand on Gisele's shoulder and with another hand quieted her. Then, taking a breath and stretching, he stood up with the help of his staff which glowed blue and purple... like a lighthouse cutting through the mirk from an obstinate, stormy sea.

With a gentle rap of his staff against the rocky ground, the light from its end illuminated a serene pool of light which reached into all the dark crannies of the ruined courtyard. Gisele gasped, it looked like the tide pools at sunset now – cast millions of different watercolors glowing with the dazzling imagination of children hard at play. There, where she knew somewhere deep in her bones the dragon ought to be, there was a tall, lanky man with splotched, murky skin. His dark eyes sunk deep into his face like whirlpools and his robes fluttered like shredded sails, ragged in the gusty breeze. Black hair ran down like scuzzy mast lines and long yellowish-white fingers poked out of sleeves which were a bit too long, suggesting the man... if ever he was... had shrunk with the years and the long exposure to brine. But the real element which caught the captain's attention was the dizzying sway of immense power which flooded out of the figure across the courtyard. Like the feeling Gisele had had as a young girl when she had foolishly climbed up on top of Oros tower's highest turret and gazed down into the foaming breakers crashing against the cliff bottom far below.

For a lingering moment, the world seemed calm and still – like the sea after squall and wind.

"Mororedros, I have come," said Romestamo, in a simple yet clear and commanding voice.

A pair of yellow, malevolent eyes flicked up at the wizard, standing amid the rubble. The dragon-in-human-form hissed. "I have nothing to say... to you or anyone else," his voice was porous and grinding, like boulders undulating into powder amid titanic waves.

Gisele looked up and fixed her eyes on Romestamo. There he stood, nearby... calm and still. A hint of lingering sorrow welled up in his eyes... like the loss of some much beloved son, claimed by the sea... sailed far away never to return into the dimming sunset over a far-stretching horizon. "You once did." said the wizard simply.

Mororedros attempted to smirk and roll his eyes... but some small part of even that vile creature hesitated... as if also haunted by some memory of a memory long ago lost to a ceaseless tide.

"Even you, here and now, can come back from the abyss you are swimming towards. Come back Mororedros – say it is not too late, my friend."

Gisele's heart broke at each word the wizard uttered. Instead of the semi-mythical legend of a man she had grown up all her life, suddenly she realized here was just a tired old man... a father calling out for a lost son.

"Wait, calling out? Wasn't Romestamo supposed to be a mute?" the captain wondered.

"Going back?!" the serpent laughed... cold and deep... from the very bottom of the impossible depths.

The captain shivered violently. The creature's mirth was far worse than its rage.

Romestamo only waited calmly... expectantly... as if he sadly already knew his long lost messenger's choice. Still, the wizard whispered, "Mororedros... come back before it is too late... your doom is nearing now."

Gisele had watched carefully this time. The wizards lips had not moved – but his voice came rolling and rumbling out from everywhere... it had only been a trick of her mind, assuming the sound came from his lips. His words resounded like thought – as if it was spoken word thought within her mind now made audible somehow.

The dragon huffed... then spat. Out of the man's mouth, small icy jets plunked out – splintering the already cracked paving stones at his feet.

"He always did have that nasty habit..." murmured Romestamo, recalling ages and ages past during a fair, greener time of existence. "Mororedros, your doom is almost upon you. Turn back, lost one. You were once my message of hope and promise to the people, just as I am. Return."

Gisele realized she had been holding her breath. She forced herself to exhale, "why doesn't the serpent just turn back into his regular self and attack Romestamo?" the captain wondered curiously.

Another closer look at Mororedros gave her a hint at the answer... The dragon was trying to furiously focus... each time the beast blinked; he had begun to smoke slightly. Wisps of Mororedros' previous frozen deluge wafted off of him, but he remained firmly man-like. The wyvern roared in frustration. "Release me, old man. I am the tides... I am the depths! I AM THE SEA!"

Romestamo gripped his staff, which blazed like a star, as he furrowed his bushy eyebrows in concentration. "Mororedros, turn back! Your doom is at the door now!"

"I AM THE SEA AND THE OCEAN ITSELF!" the dragon called, his voice chanted, louder and louder.

"TURN, MY FRIEND... TURN NOW!" Romestamo pleaded – his whole voice boomed throughout the courtyard.

Countless memories swirled, shared by both man and monster... the first day of the dragon's life. How the wizard had held the little lizard close and quieted all his simple fears. How the day Mororedros was named had also been the same day Romestamo had finally succeeded in teaching him how to breathe his own watery flames... the wizard had choked at the dragons' comic antics, shooting up out of the tide pools and spluttered his drink. Mororedros had imitated him without thinking... and out roared the blue flames! The day the dragon had learned how to dive deep – and how worried Romestamo had been... The day when Romestamo and his other wizard companion had been formally sent out by decree on their perilous ambassadorship... and how Mororedros had snuck along, following their journey by wave and sky until finally being discovered... How Romestamo had tearfully told him to return home... how Mororedros wasn't ready yet... their resulting separation and lonely wandering had been the wizard's most painful moment, excluding the current one... Romestamo could still see the dark 'v' of Mororedros soaring into the last dying embers of the sun the day they had parted ways – etched in silhouette like a rune carved along the horizon.

Mororedros, however, could barely remember the last time he had seen Romestamo. In the twinkling of a moment, the dragon cast his mind back ages upon ages... whole realms flicked by like the turning of novel's pages. Some tiny, infinitesimal sliver of him protested his own villainy. Somewhere deep down within the dragon's own labyrinthine conciseness... within the vault-like dungeons where Mororedros had hoarded his plundered treasures in the spacious room where his heart used to beat instead... he still missed the wizard. The thought was immediately shouted down and reasoned away – like the pathetic buzzing of an annoying fly. Mororedros had momentarily forgotten even the restraining spell Romestamo was casting on him – preventing him from reverting to true dragon form. The invisible coils of magical energy – stronger than triple-fold steel – while taut appeared to be only just holding. For a moment, Mororedros, Romestamo, and Gisele's collective breath held together like weird white mist, mingling in the unnatural ether all around them.

...

Prince Janos knew it when he found it. The right place... the right time. It's surprising just how many people, over goodness only knows how many years, are oblivious to situational gravity. Knowing exactly when and where you need to be... sometimes a prominent moment only comes once in a lifetime... for others, it's a rainy Tuesday afternoon at 4:57 pm. At any rate, Prince Janos knew he was exactly where and when he needed to be when the ghosts suddenly faded away. There, up ahead, was an imposing figure of a man standing before a broken archway. The prince had read more or less the right sorts of books growing up, so he knew a dragon in human form when he saw one.... Janos remembered what felt like a hundred years ago when he had read his fairytales... Dragons in human form... they looked funny. They were always described with a looming, larger-than-life sort of presence. Their skin was tinted, hinting at whatever inner nature they tended to take after and their eyes tended to retain a hypnotic, dragonish glint and cat-like slits.

When he finally entered the rubble-strewn courtyard, Janos couldn't have recalled when he had drawn his silver sword or when his mind had zeroed in on the dragon. The prince couldn't have calculated the weight of rage or crushing sense of vengeance he was more than entitled to... Couldn't have counted the faces of sorrowful ghosts or numbered the glinting silvery sparkles in his departed sister's eyes. The one thing Janos could remember was just something silly... it was the simple smell of Gisele's long, curly raven-black hair. The few days they had spent together flowed into one conscience dream. Janos remembered the walking in Trennin orchards with her... remembered her eyes watching him... remembered their time in the dark, secluded escape tunnels in the bowels of Tower Oros... So even after his boots halted a few tentative yards away from the dragon, who appeared to be straining against invisible bonds, Prince Janos's dead heart felt full to bursting with a longing he had never felt before.

A lone cry riding high on another wind far beyond the lowly airs of earth ripped by...

"TURN, MORGREDROS! THE TIME IS ALMOST UPON YOU..."

Mororedros shook his head... trying his best to beat the insolent words of his old master from his withered mind and scaly heart. "I am the sea... I am the SEA..." he muttered over and over, sometimes with conviction while other times wondering, questioning... wavering.

Prince Janos wondered why the creature had not turned to meet him yet. Finally, taking a deep breath and readying his ornate sword, he said, "dragon, you are called upon by the Prince of the Grey Isle, by the favor of the gods and by the consent of the common families, by Rumunjia and Justice herself, to pay for your crimes with your life... what say you?"

The dragon blinked again... fighting inside to squelch a different voice which burned with a tiny flaring candle of guilt and shame. "I... AM the sea..."

"What say you?" Prince Janos cried. He could feel his mind, already filled with memories of Gisele, mix with a burning sense of justice. Inside, an incredible longing began to build which went on and on...both rising, surging like the tide before a nor'wester storm, the kind of which has been known to thrash and ravage the barren western slopes of the Grey Isle at times.

For a moment Mororedros said nothing. In a cold, chill voice more icy than the darkest depth, he finally turned and said, "… with my life…pay… with my life…" There was a momentous pause… and then the dragon chuckled. The broken stones rattled with his dark mirth. Leaning towers crumbled and burning gates shivered into ash. The dragon gave one last glance over at the wizard who had been his master and friend… once upon a time. To the end of his days, Romestamo always wondered if he had spied an inkling of sad longing in his old friend's eyes then.

Then, huffing with monstrous intensity over each word, Mororedros said, "I… AM… THE… SEA!" With his last syllable, the dragon stretched all his muscled sinews, which had as of yet been coiled like cold steel, and shredded Romestamo's considerable, though ultimately pathetic magical bonds. With a roar which shook the island, he transformed back into his true form! Whirls of ash and sea spray whipped through the courtyard with the force of a hurricane. "I AM THE SEA!" boomed the dragon once more.

Janos had ducked only just in time. The dragon soared past him. In awe, the prince watched as the legendary sea serpent circled once… twice… thrice around the shattered keep before baring back down on him with a jet of lighting-blue flames. The creature's withering torrents of fire would have leveled any other ordinary man… but Prince Janos of the Grey Isle, last of his name, was not an ordinary man. As the firestorm licked his body, Janos felt his crazed mirth rising as his own inner darkness and will met and became as one. Apparently, self-preservation was high on both of their lists today.

The prince laughed and spit, unintentionally mimicking the dragon's earlier action in turn. Today was a good day for dragon slaying.

High above the wyvern blinked. Not only was his puny foe still standing… he was… laughing?

A tingling shiver ran from the tip of his snout to the last scale on Mororedros' tail. It had been an age since he had even remembered fear. The dragon didn't like it – it made him hungry... even after a thoroughly enjoyable romp through an imperial capital... and that was saying something. The wyvern snarled and dived, aiming to crush his insolent opponent. But halfway down his decent, Mororedros could feel his titanic form shifted aside – smashed by some herculean mountain of force. Taken off balance, he crashed into jumbled streets and splintered homes... leveling what presumably must have once been the market district. Out of the corner of one Mororedros' large, cat-like eyes, he saw a blazing flash of sea-blue. "Romestamo!" the dragon mentally cursed, as he shook off the remains of a barn roof. After a titanic sneeze caused by the raining chicken feathers which had exploded out from under him, Mororedros turned once more to face his tiny challengers.

A searing shock of pain leaked out from the wyvern's starboard flank. The sea serpent whipped his long neck around. There was that same insufferable prince, raising his glittering sword up for another deep plunge into his side. But what really enraged Mororedros – what really got him, was that idiotic grin the prince had the whole while... as if he were far away... or in love. The dragon roared so loud it really ought to have exploded Janos' eardrums... and perhaps it did. But either way, the prince sunk his blade deep into the dragon's slick scales once more before being thrown clean through a nearby wall.

As Janos was flying through the air, strange idle thoughts floated through his mind like luminescent willow-o-the-wisps... "I just stabbed the sea dragon... huh... hey! HEY! I JUST STABBED THE SEA DRAGON... TWICE!"

SMASH.

By all rights, the prince really ought to have been dead by now... even if he had somehow miraculously survived sea-fire from a dragon... and had not been crushed by a dragon... or not had his brain turned to a milky-grey puddle by a dragon's roar... that sturdy wall, which had once belonged to the local mason's guild, really ought to have ended him. But that's the tricky thing with undead creatures... and a rather under-appreciated fact about them: they can survive a hell of a lot of punishment, and still stand up again, very little worse for wear.

Before Mororedros could adequately investigate the fate of the prince, something flicked the side of his face, scoring his snout. Romestamo had not been idle. After doing his best to shove the dragon off his hurtling flight path, the wizard had leapt down from his rocky perch and conjured without really thinking. (A rather dangerous, but in these particular circumstances, forgivable move) Up out of the end of the blue enchanter's staff sprouted a long foaming lash which the older man could whip around with surprising intensity and accuracy. Continuing without thinking, Romestamo flung back his staff and set his whip snapping towards Mororedros as strong as he could.

SNAP!

The wizard scored his well-aimed hit right along the dragon's snout – only inches away from one of its glowing yellow eyes. Those same eyes swiveled Romestamo's way in surprise. The wizard gasped. It wasn't the full hypnotic fury of those entrancing eyes bearing down on him... or the rush of malevolence he now felt pelting his spirit... it was that Romestamo had hit his friend. He had scarred the dragon he had raised from infancy – scored the faithful adventurer who had doggedly stuck with him through countless perils – the one with whom the wizard had gone far beyond there and back again... They had seen the ends of the earth together – watched the hidden lines of the world fade away until all the sky becomes a new one and the old pillars of the sun pass away into realms hitherto unknown and unseen, except by them, together as one.

Romestamo dropped his staff with a clatter. The slithering blue whip instantly disappeared.

Mororedros appeared as equally surprised as Romestamo. For a moment, neither spoke... and then, "I will not fight you, friend." said the wizard... quietly at first, as if wondering at his own words pouring out of his heart and up through his mouth. "I will not fight you. Not even here, amid your own ruinous shame, dear one." The inaudible words shook the ground, as if some divine edict had just been decreed... and who knows, perhaps then it really had been.

The dragon cocked his head. It had been an old movement he had learned from watching little puppies make after seeing things they didn't really understand. Mororedros snarled... more at himself for his childish reaction than anything else. "You... will *not* fight me?" the dragon murmured, utterly perplexed. All around them a city lay in desolate waste. Nearly an entire people had been slaughtered. Even now – the wyvern's undead Mer allies were invading the coast lands, cutting off all escape and hope... and this wizard, bound by word and purpose to resist darkness wherever he found it, would not fight him?!

Romestamo only shook his tired, sad face and sat down in a heap. The outward guise of the legendary wizard fell away, leaving only a haggard wanderer in its place. Hot tears rolled down his face. "I won't... and I can't..." the older man tried to wipe away the staining tears and snot from his face... but it was no good... more simply came to replace them. The wizard looked up into the incredulous gaze of the sea serpent and sighed, "You're still my friend, you know. You always will be, Mororedros."

The dragon had had as much as he could take. Roaring, he shot his neck out until his massive jowls were mere feet away from the prostrate wizard. "... and what, pray tell, is to stop me from eating you right now, then, eh? You'll fail. You'll utterly fail your mission, you miserable old fool!"

"Perhaps... But I will not have failed you."

Those words smote Mororedros more than any magic silver swords ever could have. They stung deeper than any black arrow could ever have been shot. They singed greater than any poison could have ever tasted. He staggered back, involuntarily shifting back into his dizzying human-like form. There the great sea serpent stood, stricken dumb more thoroughly than the mightiest of spells could ever have smote him.

Stones skittered down from where the wizard had previously been standing. A small figure quietly walked up next to Romestamo and put a hand on his shoulder. Two perilously keen eyes glittered back through tears. "I'll fight you," she said.

Mororedros' eyes widened and then a well-practiced smirk slid back onto his face. "Go back to your piled stones and endless, futile night watches, little captain. It is over."

Captain Gisele Perrault of House Brutajia swept out her sword. Its sharp ringing, metal on metal, shattered the courtyard's stillness, "I watch not for myself..."

"But for others," masonry shifted away to their right. Up through the smoking dust and hot grey ash, stood the Prince of the Grey Isle and his eyes blazed with an infernal light.

Mororedros glanced bewildered between his two opponents, hesitating. His glowing gaze finally settled back on his former master, more out of many ages of repeated practice than anything else.

"Go... do what you must do. My love will always follow you, my friend." said Romestamo in his silent, ethereal voice, as he slowly got to his feet with the help of his staff.

For once in his long life, the dragon was at an utter loss as to what to do. His inner fire went colder than the sea's crushing depths. Still, Mororedros' lingering malice screamed for blood. With a heavy sigh like an endless evening surf, the dragon readied to slaughter the trio where they stood. But just before he unleashed his onslaught, Mororedros froze. As silent at fluttering silken curtains, the pale form of a mournful ghostly girl appeared where nothing had been before. Her haunting eyes accused him with her endless sadness. The wyvern grimaced, but did not back away. But then another ghost materialized, one with a flickering crown of pale gold and a kingly expression... and then yet another of a beautiful lady with imperious eyes and a highborn face... all so sad... all so longing. Another and another... they came here and there amid the quiet stones... cracked and fading. Men... soldiers... butchers... tailors... honest faces, questioning and unafraid... only so heart-breakingly sad. Women, eerily ravishing after all the cares of this world had fallen away from their silently shining faces. Children, taken too young from the bright world of the living, were gazing up with shattered innocence. And for a spell, the entire ghostly crowd lingered in the late and quickly fading day... murky with smoldering ash and grey sea winds ever tinged with salt. And then the dragon fled like an evil ghost in the patchy sunshine. With a desperate furl of his long cloak, Mororedros transformed into a brisk sea-breeze and shot away into the north, never to be seen in the Grey Isle again.

THE END

Epilogue

L egends tell of the whalers far in the utter northern reaches, retold by the Wisemen of the Isles of the Sea Kings, of the rushing winds between the floating icebergs. How on dark October nights, when the wind is in the east and the lanterns have all burned low, the roaring voice of one rushes through the icy canyons and over the dark blue of the waves. And if you are quiet enough and listen hard... you can still hear the voice of the terrible sea serpent of the Grey Isle, endlessly crying and whispering over the waves. No longer a creature able to haunt the physical world of men, they say the great sea wyvern Mororedros is little more than spirit, haunted by the ghosts of that lost people, the Rumenjians of the Grey Isle, and endlessly pursued by the greatest terror of all: his own shame which follows him wherever he goes... for Mororedros knows his wizard still loves him, and will never stop doing so – even beyond the ending of the worlds.

As for Prince Janos Ulian and Captain Gisele Perrault, little is now known or remembered. But when the six great Rillian ships landed on the Dardan coasts, those of the Blue Lord who explored northward up along the shore, they discovered the remains of a sturdy sea-fort. There it stood, built up from abandoned docks often found among the wild, scattered fisher-folk along that barren way. Etched into the abandoned gateways made for smaller men than Rillians, was the great eagle sigil of House Ulian, intertwined with the bear of House Brutajian. To this day, two of the major star constellations are even called The Prince and The Captain – who shine brightest during the dark endings of late autumn months, and dance across the crisp, frozen skies... united forever as they hunt The Great Dragon constellation at the death of each year.

Q&A

1. *Where was Romestamo when the sea dragon attacked the first time?*

Good question! Romestamo has been hunting for his dragon ever since he and his other wizard friend, Morren, were separated while coming to this story's world. During the events of the story, Romestamo was, similarly to Avors and Janos, on to the undead conspiracy, which ultimately brought about Rumenjia's destruction on the Isle. And like the Prince and the Legate, was too late to save everyone. Knowing that Romestamo would head straight towards the capital once the attack began outright, Mororedros placed special units of undead soldiers to surprise and capture the wizard once he arrived. Thanks to Janos and Gisele's efforts, Romestamo was later freed and went immediately onwards with them to try and still stop the dragon. Notice that the sea dragon could have just had the wizard killed outright - but even then, something inside Mororedros prevented him from doing so.

2. *Why did the sea dragon want to attack the land in the first place?*

Well... somethings are still secret-secret until the third volume of *Rienspel* releases. But I can tell you that the undead conspiracy is not limited to the Grey Isle alone; and also that the undead are tricky and deadly smart. There is a reason for everything they do. Thinking of them as mindless zombies or careless, blood-crazed demons means seriously underestimating their ultimate goal for the world...

3. *What is the connection with House* Scypiasia *and the sea dragon? Why do they join forces? Does House* Scypiasia *want to overthrow the kingdom too?*

For part of this answer – see above. As for specifically why members of House Scypiasia and the sea dragon join forces - it's actually because there's two major things going on which most can really only guess at. First, the undead are quite tolerant about who joins their ranks - they really do want everyone to join their one big happy family in the end... or die... either way suits them just fine. Secondly, the Scypiasians are actually on to the undead, too. You can't orchestrate a massive take over like that and not raise some eyebrows. The Prince and the Legate are on to the undead. The wizard is on to the dragon and the undead. AND House Scypiasia are on to the undead. Unfortunately, the Rumenjian House falsely assumed the Prince was leading the undead since he himself is undead... sort of. The undead thrive in conditions like this. Wherever there is fear and suspicion - hate and prejudice - the Undead thrive. And House Scypiasia fell right for it, especially since they've been jealous of House Ulian for generations. Later, in stories I'll get to eventually, back in Rumenjia proper on the other side of the mainland – there is a massive civil war going on during *Rienspel* between the same three houses, which the undead are blatantly playing off each other... but, I'm getting ahead of myself.

4. *How much time takes place between the Prince's royal ball and the beginning of the story?*

Oh... if I had to guess... at least 10 years or more... I roughly imagined Janos to be in his low to mid 30's...

5. *When did Prince Janos's parents die?*

Excellent question! If I hadn't mentioned already, *The Grey Isle Tale* is actually one of the oldest (for me) stories I ever outlined for this world. It actually began to take place during my very first attempts at writing *Rienspel*. Back then, I was writing so many different story ideas I was losing track of everything! My wife, Steph, told me, pick one story and work on it. *The Grey Isle Tale*, in some possible alternate universe, I conceivably could have selected it to labor on first, instead of *Rienspel*... I say all this because in my first outline, one of the things one discovers is that the king actually fights the dragon, one on one, throughout the castle. The flashes the trio see as they near the burning citadel when they first come to it is actually Mororedros battling the king after the queen was killed. The ghosts you see as Janos makes his way through the city are, largely, *fresh* ghosts. When the spirit of his sister says 'mother and father are coming'... she's being literal. They are just then coming.

6. *I get the impression the king and queen were alive when Janos was stabbed. Then why was he assassinated if he wasn't king? Or why wasn't the king assassinated first?*

Another great question! Janos' parents were alive after he was stabbed. The undead, as you recall, like to work this way. They love turning mother against father - son against sister - child against parent. They love manipulating events so that people don't just die or get turned - they want people to hate each other and kill each other; similar to Tolkien's ring wraiths, their power is with fear and death, hate and cowardliness. More damage to the realm was done by attempting to turn Janos then potentially ever could have with just the king... The whole Scypiasian paranoia spun out of it, in the end.

7. *Is there anything significant to the sickness that the princess died of?*

You know, I honestly didn't think about it when writing - but I suspect there was. The king and queen don't sound particularly nice whenever Janos remembers them earlier on. But some of that is because his memories are being purposefully manipulated by the evil spirit within him... I can only imagine, with all the general exposure to the undead, sickness comes too. When people cease treating each other with kindness and goodness - all sorts of evil arises. Just like in the old Celtic stories - when the people are good, the land is good... and likewise, when the people are wicked the land turns bad... it's a telling real-life example of active magic in our world, today, I think.

7. *Did you think of anything else about Janos' necklace that didn't get into the story?*

Maybe... I don't want to get too ahead of myself, again, though. All I will say is that evil things usually cannot stand Circles. You'll actually find out a bit more about Circles in the current work I'm writing - *The Last Circle*, which, among other things, is all about The Fall and the effects of its aftermath in this world.

8. Did you make up any more information about what happens after death / ghosts? You mention giving coins to a ghost for them to cross the river...

You know, a funny thing happens when you read great classical works... you are exposed to all these great, classical ideas. No, I did not make up that information. It's right in *The Aeneid*, by Virgil, heralding from all the way back to Ancient Greece. You can Wikipedia Hades and read more about it there, or read the book. It's actually why, in my opinion, many Catholics, even to this day, still place coins over the eyes of their dead... they may claim it's for different reasons... but I believe the practice is still a direct hand-over from antiquity. The River is Styx... although, it is also interesting, if you think about, that even the Bible mentions a River (the River of Life) as something people cross over in the book of Revelation. And... as you asked, I also took some of this part from personal near death experiences... not so much the river or coin parts, though...

9. What happened to the cohorts who were part of the group who wanted to assassinate Janos while he was inspecting the Tower Oros?

They were Scypiasians who were attempting to kill Janos because he was undead. Little did they realize that, apparently, there is undead, and then there is UNDEAD. Also, there was more going on than just a straight undead power-play (there almost always is a ton more going on). The cohorts took Tower Oros, but it was all for naught. They killed their own countrymen for nothing. Janos and Avors escaped, and the attackers created a dangerous enemy with Captain Gisele. *Additionally*, the whole order to attack Tower Oros was really just a giant, ruse to get as many actual non-undead soldiers away from the capital, so when that evening came, and the dragon assaulted the citadel, very few loyal soldiers would be there to protect it. The next day, when Rumenjia on the Grey Isle had fallen, Avor's men came to the towers and tried to warn the occupying Scypiasians about what had happened. Those who listened deserted their cohort and evacuated... those who didn't were eventually overwhelmed.

10. Was the point of assassinating Janos to gain control over him? Did the Undead know the necklace would prevent him from being possessed?

Again, some of this was answered previously. No, no they didn't. The undead are not all-knowing... as much as they'd like to have you believe otherwise. They have limitations and do make mistakes..., which sometimes end up being rather critical errors, at times. In addition, unless I blatantly say something was destroyed, it's probably still floating around some unexpected corner of my world... (Just so you know...)

Ready for more from Ryan P. Freeman?
Check out the teaser for
The Phoenix of Redd, Volume I: Rienspel
Coming Fall 2016!

What Rien discovers about his past will change his future...

Rien Sucat wiles his days away, bored-stiff in his small backwoods village. But soon gets more than he bargained for after he befriends a magical Phoenix, accidentally witnesses a secret necromantic ritual, and comes face to face with a league of racist, knife-wielding assassins out for his blood. Travel with Rien as he and the Phoenix journey from the unassuming Rillian village of Nyrgen through the enchanting depths of the Great Wood where the unquiet dead lurk, to the high north country of Firehall - elusive sanctuary of the Elves. Launch into an epic quest with consequences farther reaching than Rien could ever possibly imagine.

Rienspel is about heart. It is about family and about how the power of love played out in everyday life often carries lasting consequences. Rien's tale transcends the dim shadows of our own world by revealing the lingering power we all carry through how we live and treat others. It is a tale about the Story we all reside in which readers both young and young-at-heart will find compelling. As C.S. Lewis once penned for his colleague and friend J.R.R. Tolkien, so it is with *Rienspel*, 'here are beauties which pierce like swords or burn like cold iron. Here is a story which will break your heart"... and re-forge it anew in Phoenix-fire.

Chapter I

From Darkness to Light

A tall figure sped through dense woods at twilight. The sound of pursuit – monstrous footfalls – came crashing only a breath behind. Honed arrows whizzed by. Dull thuds indicated where they deeply embedded themselves in thick-grained forest trees. The fleeing boy's heart pounded like a master smith's forge.

Crash Crash Crash

He had wandered too far from firelight and now he was paying for it. His vision blurred with sweat... luckily, he knew the woods infinitely better than his persistent hunters did. Leaves whirled by in reds, browns, and yellows streaking wild pale light through curling, heady mist. The forest shadows grew, ushering an ominous night. The boy wished he were indoors, safe behind strong stone walls or around a bright bonfire... because he knew sinister things lurked in the woods after sunset. And now they were after him.

Because of what he was...

"There is no escape Woodspirit! There is no more pretending among the true Sons of Poseidon!" The ringing voice was high and piercing, and somehow vaguely familiar to the fleeing figure. The heavy footfalls charged ceaselessly on with an unsteady, lurching pattern, crushing underbrush as it passed.

The boy dodged into a thick hollow of trees, hoping to hide in the gathering tendrils of mist. His lungs burned - tempting his mind to surrender to whatever grim fate the hunters intended. Vaguely, the boy began wishing for his familiar village and his mother... for the girl he would probably never see again... and for his brother.

The boy's last thought forced him to shudder... remembering the cold, fell light kindled in his older brother's eyes the last night they ever saw each other...

The boy peered around the massive oak trunk he had taken refuge behind. Just across the moonlit glade, one of his hunters, a man ten feet tall and clad all in dark green and leather cast his gaze here and there, relentlessly searching. The same fell, maniacal light seemed to glow out of the hulking figure's hazel eyes the boy's brother had, once upon a time.

The lean boy shivered again.

"Rien Sucat, you are summoned by her majesty the Emerald Queen to face your crimes against Rillium. Surrender." The glimmering light glinted off a trident-shaped broach.

Using the brief halt to gulp the nippy air, Rien wheezed, trying to regain his breath. Glancing left, he thought he saw a long, stretching hollow between the intertwining bows of gargantuan trees and immediately bolted noiselessly away.

A cry rang out within the sylvan depths, "You cannot flee forever, Sucat! We know what you are!"

The moon, looming and perilously bright, peaked far above an eastern aspen speckled ridge. Glimmering through the shivering, pale, golden leaves, the shafts illuminated the long, northerly natural tunnel which Rien stumbled into. In the shadowy distance, the sounds of the hunters seemed to be slowly fading away to the south. Idly, the panting boy wondered what his friends, the other rangers and General Fy'el, would think when he did not return.

Would they miss him?

Or merely continue their desperate errand to restore justice and peace to a kingdom who had banished them within the forest depths they had once protected. Already the boy desperately wished he had not decided to wander from the rangers' camp earlier that day.

The heavy footfalls were not close anymore, but they weren't far either... Rien wrapped his tattered grey cloak around him to ward off the pooling mist and fall chill and began trotting northwards, following the hollow through the trees. Soon the forest's night sounds began to sing softly again as the moon climbed higher in the late October sky. Coloured leaves crunched under the boy's soft, supple boots as he nimbly advanced into the uncharted woodland depths. Soon his racing imagination began to wind down - and slowly the once frightening tree shadows resumed their old friendly, watchful repose.

With another step, Rien's boots stumbled over a half-buried paving stone, almost entirely hidden by leaves and mossy dirt. He swiveled his head south down the long, narrow tree hollow and then back towards the looming north, to the darkling, snow-capped mountains dimly reflecting the moon and starlight. Judging it was now safe, or as safe as it ever was in the Great Forest these days, the boy threw himself onto a nearby hazel stump.

"I must be on some kind of road" he thought as he scraped the loose soil and leaves away with his boots, revealing a worn road.

If he had not been dog-tired, sore and hunted, Rien would have been immensely curious. On either side of what he thought must once have been a spacious road there looked like round white stones lining the way. The trees grew close all around him, and something in the tall boy told him they were up to something. Whenever the wind blew through the branches the creaking sounded like whispering, but for good or for evil Rien could not tell.

"I mean you no harm, old Hazel and Ash." He muttered softly.

But only a Borean wind breathed through the branches and broad, crackly leaves, which floated lazily down on the crumbling road. The boy picked up one of the round, white, lining stones lying forlornly near him and examined it. Its surface was smooth, yet pitted and scoured with ageless years of pedestrian service to who knew where. It reminded Rien of the Trivulet pillars near his home. An image of the three white pillars standing firmly where the three forest rivers met near his village, Nyrgen, flashed like lightning in his head. But he quickly pushed the painful thoughts from his fatigued mind and pulled out his water skin and swallowed a mouthful of shockingly cold water. Momentarily refreshed, he stood up, stretched, and resumed walking northwards. As he labored, his searching eyes would often spot dim trees blooming with crimson flowers occasionally dotting the woodland away to his distant left.

Rien trudged onwards, wondering out loud if he would ever find Firehall, the elusive sanctuary he had been desperately seeking ever since late summer. But now autumn was waning fast and the place was beginning to seem like only a fading dream - intangible like the thick, blanketing mist in the hollows swirling all around him now, nebulous and hidden, untouchable.

The trees were becoming larger, something barely conceivable in the Great Forest, where the average trunk was twice the length of a man's reach. Rien's breath was now visible in the cold air, and he was just beginning to think how nice a fire would be again when a flickering light abruptly appeared up ahead.

The boy was not stupid though.

It could be anything... and with his luck it belonged to some sinister figure who only meant him harm. Or... or it was an old friend...

Rien weighed the odds, and finally decided to investigate. Hope of friends looking for him suddenly blazed up in his heart. As silent as a shadow, he slipped off the ancient path and into the innumerable trees. Stalking towards the light, Rien made sure to fix in his mind which way the path was - just in case he needed to quickly find it again. All living creatures in the wood were blissfully oblivious to the youth's swift passing as he went along.

Soon, Rien could make out distinct flames surrounded by many figures dancing round and round, laughing and calling in a wild, jovial tongue. Encircling the grove was ring of trees like he had seen distantly away to the left earlier, all checkered with bright crimson flowers, now luminous in the flickering firelight. Sitting on what appeared to be a fantastic throne grown out of a massive, living hazel tree sat a beautiful young elfess - as fair as the moon and as lovely as summer's sunset. She wore a long flowing robe and matching tunic which seemed to stream like iron-grey rain edged in cloudy white. Her mantle was sable and upon her head she wore a delicate crown of lithe silver and tiny twinkling emeralds. Her long strawberry-red hair tumbled down a little ways past her shoulders and her dark blue eyes blazed brightly. But Rien thought she looked rather bored, despite the rollicking dance which whirled all around her. The others, all elves of varying dress, seemed to be always keeping half an eye on the enthroned girl... waiting for something which the spellbound boy could not puzzle out.

Tearing his gaze away, Rien saw a handsome young elf sigh and gaze longingly at the elfess, and then retire near a large flagon, joining a throng of elves.

They started toasting his health and joking in their fluid, breathy voices and he smiled weakly... but always his eyes were on the girl... and Rien thought he heard him whisper "Aelhuin... Aelhuin... Balla Vair..."

Transfixed, Rien watched as the hundreds of dancers paused their singing and laughing and dancing and feasting in the blink of an eye: for the red-haired elfess had chosen a dancing partner at last.

Right on cue, the dazzling girl floated towards the elf. She said something in her graceful, playful tongue to the whispering elf. It seemed to Rien the elf suitor was transformed, he stood up straight and his whole face beamed a wide, soft smile. All the dazed elf could manage was an inaudible, muttered reply as she led him nearer to the fire and they began dancing together.

Rien at once understood their dance, for it was a simple one. Yet, he admitted, it was the most graceful flow of two bodies he had ever seen. They did not simply dance, they almost seemed to understand each other's souls through how they moved - at times floating as one, at others, as two separate, yet complimentary melodies. They appeared almost seamless, as if they were one pulsing mind and one throbbing heart. It was half way through their dance before Rien even realized there was music being played or even the hundreds of other couples dancing alongside them as well.

And then one single shocking realization made Rien's whole lithe frame numb.

He knew her.

Or, at least he had seen her before... many months ago before he left Nyrgen. The memory spilled back into his mind like warm sunshine. He could still see her pale, delicate hand reaching out of the shadows to pick a flower the shape of a king's crown during last midsummer's eve. His heart seemed to stop. The rest of the memory was a nightmare he never wished to recall again... a memory which still haunted him... full of death and slaughter and shame... a cold terror which Rien could neither conceal nor forget.

But there she was - radiant and glowing, breathtakingly beautiful - her red hair wreathed with silver flowers and colourful fall leaves. And for a moment, the stark memories left him for the first time, and the night terrors faded.

He exhaled, relieved, his eyes glittering out of the forest depths.

All the dancers froze.

Every eye was on him, including hers.

With one hand motion, she sent the many guards away - the elves who had suddenly conjured themselves, fully armed, out of thin air; and with a second motion she summoned the boy out of the deep shadows.

Rien's heart beat even faster than when the hunters had chased him.

But step by shaky step he stumbled through the trees. The boy hesitated on the edge of the firelight, suddenly afraid. Afraid of what he was... and of who all the merry elves might assume he was. A Rillian. A Terros. One sworn to kill elves. A tyrant and a butcher and, and...

And then suddenly she was standing before him.

A trembling light shone out of her as she beheld this tall, gaunt ranger. A long sword was by his side, and a bow and quiver were slung across his broad shoulders. His young, tender face held fear and wonder and shame all at once, but in his eyes and his heart, she sensed no shadow. She reached beyond the fire's glow and grasped his rough hand within the darkness, and led him into the light...

...

For more from Ryan Freeman – watch for the first instalment of the upcoming Trilogy, *The Phoenix of Redd, Volume I: Rienspel*
– coming Fall 2016

Acknowledgements

I would like to thank all the usual crowd for this one... First for my wife Steph, whose unfailing constructive criticism has leveled whole kingdoms, and made the world all the better for it. Secondly, a big thank-you goes out to my stalwart beta-readers, Josiah Bohn, Robert Dean, and Jennie Kelly. Without whose timely advice and sagely input, my stories would be far more frail and timid creatures. And finally, I'd like to thank all the wonderful folks over at the St. Louis Writer's Guild, who patiently answered one wanna-be-author's questions during a steam-punk festival and who continually put up with an out-of-towner's shenanigans. *Thank You, all.*

Also, I would like to thank you (*yes, you*), dear reader, I think Shakespeare's Puck said it best when he said:

> *"If we shadows have offended,*
> *Think but this, and all is mended,*
> *That you have but slumbered here*
> *While these visions did appear.*
> *And this weak and idle theme,*
> *No more yielding but a dream,*
> *Gentles, do not reprehend:*
> *If you pardon, we will mend:*
> *And, as I am an honest Puck,*
> *If we have unearned luck*
> *Now to 'scape the serpent's tongue,*
> *We will make amends ere long;*
> *Else the Puck a liar call;*
> *So, good night unto you all.*
> *Give me your hands, if we be friends,*
> *And Robin shall restore amends."*

About the Author

Ryan P. Freeman is a fellow adventurer. After miraculously surviving childhood cancer, he launched into talk radio. Ryan is a pastor, former International Red Cross speaker, and medieval-enthusiast; loves sampling craft-beers, and is an unapologetically proud kilt-wearer. His interests range from exploring real-world pan-mythology, to survivalist camping and copious video gaming. Ryan also writes for *The Scribe*, an online literary magazine based out of St Louis.

Made in the USA
San Bernardino, CA
24 June 2019